Let Me Love You

Amy Davies

Zara
#StayWilde

<u>Dedications</u>

First off, I would like to thank my awesome husband, who has stuck by me through the whole book, even when I hit a huge writer's block. He has taken care of our 3 children and even cooked
Thank you to my family and friends that supported me.
Darryl I love you babe, just keep being you always and Thank you for letting me love you.
My 3 children you give me the inspiration every day. I love you lots like jelly tots.
Also a huge Thank you to some amazing girls that I have met online. Ladies you are my Rock stars.
Kim, Kellie, Kaz, Sarah and Carolyn, Toski and Carrie. I love you chicas

Contact details: amydaviesbooks@gmail.com
Twitter account - @AmyDaviesAuthor
Facebook.com/AmyDaviesBooks

Cover rights are owned by Toski Covey Photography
Edited by Kellie Montgomery

Let Me Love You

Prologue

It's Friday night and yet again I'm alone, but these days I like being alone. No one's here to see the bruises, or the way he speaks to me. The apartment is clean, just the way he likes it; it doesn't take me long these days, as it's easier to keep on top of everything. I take my e-reader out of my bag and sit in the bay window looking over the city. I'm reading a book about a very hot CEO dominant that actually takes care of his girl and loves her. My dominant boyfriend just likes to hit and rape me. Where did I go wrong with that? I wish I could just leave, but he has threatened to kill my family and I know that both he and his dad have the means to do it. He reminds me daily that he has this power over me.

I hear the front door unlock and my hearts jumps in my throat. I hear the laughter of him and two others. Oh God, he has brought Dylan and Evan back with him. This is not going to be a good night. "Tally, where are you?!" I hear Dean shout.

I plaster a fake smile on my face and reply. "I'm by the bay window, Dean. You guys have a good night?" All three men stroll into our living room. They sway back and forth, I can tell they are all drunk.

"You guys have a good night?"

"Come here Tally" Dean demands. "Greet our guests in the proper manner."

I steady my shaky breath and move towards them. I stop and kiss Dylan on the cheek.

"How have you been Dyl?" He smiles a creepy smile that always makes my skin crawl.

"I'm good Tally, even better now babe." I nod and move to Evan. Evan is the sweetest of the group.

"Hey Evan. How's the new job going?" I ask, as I know that he just started a new job.

"Yeah Tally, job is good. You okay?" He asks in a knowing manner.

Dean wraps his arm around my waist and pulls me closer.
"Are you done flirting with my boys, Tally? Because if you like them that much then I can think of a few ways to please them and me." He smirks.

"I wasn't flirting Dean. You asked me to come and greet them, so I did." He didn't answer me. I felt the back of his hand connect with my face and I fall to the floor.

"You really want to piss me off girl? You know you want to fuck them. I see they way you look at Evan, so get back into the guest room and strip now. My boys are horny after drinking and flirting with whores all day, so they deserve a little action. Don't you think?"

I look at Dean with horror that sinks right into my bones. "You can't make me have sex with Dylan and Evan, Dean. Please don't do this. I'm yours and only yours." I'm shaking now, tears streaming down my face.

I would take a beating before I let the three of them take me. I stand and head for the door, but get yanked back by my hair.
Dean whispers in my ear. "You will do as you're told girl, now fucking strip." He throws me toward the guest room. I steady myself and shake my head no.

"No Dean, this isn't happening. Send the boys home and you can make love to me. Please."

I plead with him, but he doesn't give in. Dean comes at me and hits me again. From the floor, I see Dylan smiling and rubbing his erection through his jeans. Evan is averting his eyes. I pray in my head that Evan will help me, put a stop to this, but he doesn't. Dean kicks me in the ribs as I try to get to my feet. He turns to the boys and smiles.

"Go into the guest room, second door on the left. We will be there in a few." I look at Evan again and mouth 'Please'. He shakes his head and follows Dylan. Evan looks just as scared as me.

"Get up! You are going to go in there and fuck my boys, okay? Dylan wants to taste that sweet pussy of yours." I cringe and begin to dry heave. I stand and look Dean in the face. I'm shaking from head to foot. I glance around the room and spot my bag sitting on the floor near the door. I have to get out of here. I can taste blood in my mouth and I'm sure I have a few broken ribs, but I'm going to have to grin and deal with the pain if I want to get out of here.

"Dean, this isn't happening tonight, or ever." He laughs at me and I feel sick to my stomach.

"Oh doll face, it is going to happen. Remember, just one phone call and you will be responsible for Scarlett and Jake getting hurt, or worse" My blood runs cold, but something snaps inside of me.

"Fuck you Dean." I pick up the vase that's to my right and throw it at Dean. It catches his shoulder, so I make a run for the door while he regains his balance from trying to dodge the vase. Dean's mom bought that vase. I fucking hate it. I fling the door open and run for the elevator. Pushing the buttons a mile a minute doesn't make the doors open any faster, but I still do it. The doors open as Dean runs out of our apartment door, screaming at me.

Oh God please, please. I will the doors to close.

The doors close as Deans gets there, but he is not fast enough. I hear him scream my name, but I block it out. I sag against the wall and collapse to the floor. Breathing heavily, I text my sister Scarlett to see if she is home. The doors slide open with a ping and I jump out of my skin; part of me was expecting Dean to be waiting for me. I stand and exit the building, feeling the evening warmth on my skin. For the first time in so many months, I feel free of the clutches of Dean Riley. I call a taxi cab and head to my sister Scarlett's place.

I Natalia Slone now welcome freedom, hopefully.

Chapter 1

My interview is in a few days with a big shot photography company named Exposure. They found one of my photos online and asked me to come in for a job interview. Why oh why did I say yes? Photography is just a hobby of mine. I have never thought of taking it further, but Scarlett my big sister, convinced me that this might be a good thing for me. My family sees this as my chance to meet Mr. Right. You never know, I might make it big. I live with Scarlett. I know I cramp her style from time to time, but I know she loves me.

"Tally, it's eight o'clock. We're going to hit traffic and be late opening the store. Get a move on!" Scarlett shouts at me from our kitchen.

I work in a small clothing boutique called Scarlett's Avenue. Scarlett owns the store. When she turned twenty-five, she got a large part of her inheritance and actually did something good with her money. Scarlett was a tad on the wild side at a younger age, but after certain events, she grew up. Scarlett's Avenue sells vintage chic style clothes with large price tags.

We will be celebrating her thirtieth birthday soon and in true Scarlett style we are having a big glitzy party. I come down the stairs to meet Scarlett at the bottom, tapping her foot, giving me a get-a-move-on-glare.

"Ok I'm here, let's get a move on, we don't want to piss off the boss." I say to her while I dance past her and head towards to door.

Scarlett scowls at me. "You're really going to wear that to work?"

I'm wearing skinny jeans with a plain black fitted shirt that buttons up to my breasts and a white camisole underneath with flats. I don't think she likes my fashion sense. I don't really have a style. I just wear whatever I feel comfortable in.

I nod and keep walking, smiling to myself. Scarlett is a very modern kind of girl, always keeping up with fashion trends and always getting the men.

Scarlett has long straight chocolate brown hair, beautiful green eyes, and according to a guy that once described her to me, legs that go all the way up. She has the perfect body. She took her looks after our mom.

Now me, well, I'm me. I have shoulder length mousey coloured hair, blue eyes, and legs that don't go all the way up, but I'm pretty slim. 'Too skinny' mom says, but I follow my dad's side of the family. We arrive at the store. We are busy, as every other day. Customers come and go, not really looking to me for any fashion advice. They just look down on me until Scarlett steps in.

I go out back on my break, check over my emails, and do some research on Exposure. They have a hand in everything, from family photos to portfolios. Their main reason for being such a big company is all the celebrity work that they do, from promo shoots to red carpet. They have pictures on their website of celebrities. I don't know most of them, as I don't watch a lot of TV or movies.

I click the slideshow and have a look at what other celebs they have photographed. As the screen is flicking through, I hit the 'stop' button. There is a guy I have never seen before. He has big blue ocean eyes and a smile that could make anyone fall in love instantly.

I tingle in all the right places. After seeing the star studded list of celebs, I start to panic. How am I never going to get this job? I'm not going to fit in here at all, and now I'm really nervous. I go back out to the front of the store where Scarlett is talking to a well dressed woman in her mid-fifties. They both stop talking and turn to look at me. Scarlett waves her hands, summoning me to them. I walk over, keeping my eye on Scarlett, who is just smiling at me.

"Natalia, this is Mrs. Silver. She owns Exposure and she has come into the store today to look for a pretty dress for her Grand-daughter, Penny. Can you help her please, Tally?" Scarlett walks away, leaving me there with Mrs. Silver. I stand there looking at this amazingly dressed woman and realize that I have lost my voice.

Great! I take a deep breath.

"How old is your Grand-daughter, Mrs. Silver and what is the occasion for the outfit? That might help on deciding the best outfit for her." Mrs Silver smiles at me.

"Penny will be sixteen and it's her sweet sixteen birthday party." You can tell that she adores her Grand-daughter by the way she smiles when she says her name.

We go looking around the racks picking out a number of dresses for the birthday girl, Penny. Mrs. Silver shows me a photo of Penny and I notice she is very pretty and tall like Scarlett. One of the dresses I pick out is a pretty ivory knee length strapless dress with a very fine silver belt at the waist. Mrs Silver loves it. *Phew.*

"Is there anything else I can help you with, Mrs. Silver?" I ask, as we head over to the counter for her to pay for her item. Mrs. Silver shakes her head and hands me her credit card. "Would you like me to gift wrap the dress for Penny?"

"Yes please, Natalia, or do you prefer Tally?" Mrs Silver asks. I look at her blush slightly for no reason.

"I like Tally. I will just go and gift wrap the dress for you." I let out a big breath as I take the dress out the back of the store to the gift wrapping station, which isn't all it cracks up to be, it's just a table with boxes, colored tissues, and ribbons.

I hand Mrs Silver the pretty white box with a pink bow and she nods and heads out of the store. As soon as Mrs Silver is out of the door, I head for Scarlett who is talking to a customer, but I don't care. I grab her arm and apologize to the customer, who looks a little confused.

"Really Scarlett? Really? What were you thinking? That could have gone so badly, do you understand that? You know I don't know much about fashion, that's why I tend to cash up or sort the stock out."

"God Tally, keep your panties on. I thought I was doing you a favor. You have been so nervous about Saturday. I thought if you were to meet the owner you could sum her up, make yourself feel better." Scarlett really does like taking care of me, but this time she really blew me away. The day pretty much goes quick, but makes me nervous, as I know that I'm closer to my interview at Exposure. While driving home, my phone beeps and my heart jumps into my throat.

Get a grip Tally' it's a job interview and Mrs Silver didn't know who you were.

I fish my phone out of my bag and check the text and I relax; it's Cassidy, my best friend. We have known each other for a few years now and she gets me. Cassidy doesn't try to change me, she loves me for me.

Cassidy: Drink's after work, meet 8.00 JAG <3

Just what I need. Tomorrow's my day off, so I'm out with my friends to take my mind off my pending interview. I take a pit stop at home. I brush my hair, add some make-up, change my clothes, and have a quick glance in the mirror. *Oh you'll do girl.* I'm now wearing my black jeans that simply hug my body and put a new white camisole. I throw my favorite blue blazer on and I'm out the door and into a waiting taxi cab.

I'm the last to arrive at JAG, which is nothing unusual. All my friends are sitting in a booth with red leather covers and a dark wood frame. The table has one single lamp in the middle, which shines up at their faces.

As I look around the table, I see my best-friend Cassidy draped over her boyfriend Josh. Next to Josh is Lucas, the "man-whore", as we like to call him. As long has the girl has boobs, he is there.

Ellie is sitting next to Marie. They are cousins, but also best friends. I smile at Lucas, who is scanning the room for his next victim. I signal that I'm going to the bar to get my drink.

I order a Southern Comfort and lemonade with ice, which is my usual drink. Dade, the barman, hands me my glass. Dade is such a sweet boy. He is all six foot hard muscle with dark hair. I chat with Dade about him getting a girlfriend, but he doesn't seem too bothered about settling down at the moment. He is just happy fooling around. Typical man.

I finish my drink and order another. While I'm chatting with Dade, I feel a hand on the small of my back. I turn to look and stop breathing. The guy that was on the Exposure website is standing next to me with his amazing sexy smile and I just melt.

"Hi, do you mind if I cut in?" I am lost for words. I can't speak. I'm just staring at him, so Dade takes over.

"Never mind her, what can I get you?" It should be illegal to look this hot. He takes his drink from Dade and slides a twenty dollar bill across the bar.

"For the lady's drink." He looks at me with an All-American-Smile "Thanks for letting me cut in. Hi, I'm James"

"I'm...T...Tally" *Oh my fucking God, get a grip Tally!*

"So Tally, are you here with friends?" I look at my friends and James follows my gaze. He smiles and bends to speak in my ear. I can feel his hot breath on my skin and my body starts to burn. "Catch you later, maybe." He winks and casually walks off.

Fuck me!!

I melt in all the right places. My body tingles from head to foot. How the hell did he do that? I watch him walk away. He looks back at me with a sexy smirk on his lips and winks again.

I look back at Dade, who is smiling at me. "What the hell is with you? It's not like you to act like that." I shake my head and get my thoughts together.

"Fuck if I know. God dude, did you see his eyes? I could get lost in them." I slow my breathing down. I join my friends at the table where the conversation is about me and the hot guy that I spoke to at the bar. Cassidy looks at me with total shock on her face "What?" I look at Cassidy.

"Tally you have no idea, do you?" I shake my head at her. I have absolutely no clue what she is talking about. "God Tally, you really should start watching some TV. That guy that spoke to you at the bar," She stops looking at me like I have grown horns. "His name is James Wilde, he is the new big thing on TV. He is in the new QBC TV show 'Control', you really have no idea?"

I look at her as if she has just given me a huge math problem. I was never good at math. I shrug it off and go sit next to Marie, who is texting on her phone yet again. She looks up at me through her long black hair which has fallen from behind her ears. She gives me a smile and goes straight back to her texting.

"So chica, when is your interview? Are you nervous yet?" Lucas asks.

"It's on Saturday at ten-thirty and yes Lucas, I'm nervous. We can't all be like you Mr. I'm cool at everything." I snap back. I don't know why I did that. It's not Lucas's fault I'm feeling like this. He looks taken back and I close my eyes. On opening them I reach for his hand. "I'm sorry Lucas, I shouldn't have snapped at you. Yes babe I'm nervous." He smiles and moves over to me.

"No worries baby." He kisses my cheek and winks at me and it's all forgotten. I look across the club and see James Wilde staring right at me with a frown on his perfect face. I look away as soon as I make eye contact. There are a few girls hanging around him, but he doesn't seem to be paying them any attention.

Chapter 2

The girls drag me onto the dance floor with Rita Ora – How We Do (Party) playing while the boys carry on with their boy talk. The music is pumping and we are all jumping and dancing and really enjoying ourselves. Cassidy is now dancing for Josh who is watching her like a hawk, but in a good way. He adores her with all of his being and I love that about them. Josh would do anything for Cassidy. I just wish I had a guy like that all to myself. We dance for most of the night and I have now removed my blazer, as it's hot in here.

The song changes and I feel an arm slip around my waist and a hard warm body pushes flush against my back. I lean into the body that's grinding into me and I grind back. The guy runs his hands up and down my arm, causing my skin to heat up. I don't know how long we dance for, as my head is swimming from the alcohol and I start to feel unsteady on my feet.

The body is hot and solid. He feels so good and Goddamn, he smells good. Marie pulls me off from the dance floor and sits me back in the red leather booth. I'm a tad drunk. It doesn't happen often, but when it does, oh boy do I pay for it the next morning.

Ellie and Marie call me a cab, as I'm in no fit state to walk, or get myself home for that matter. I share the cab with the girls, as they don't want to leave me alone. We pull up outside my house and they help me over to Scarlett, who is waiting for me. She doesn't look too pleased with me.

"What the hell Natalia? Don't you know when to stop?" Scarlett must be mad, she only uses my full first name when she is really mad. "Obviously not." She states. Scarlett is the more responsible one now.

"She was really nervous Scar, she needed to unwind." Ellie explains.

"Fine. I'll take her from here. You girls should go home, it's late." Scarlett lays down the law to my adult friends. I think she forgets that we're twenty-four. Scarlett has to help me into the house and up to my room, as everything is blurry and shifting. I bounce from side to side of the door frame of my bedroom like a human ping pong ball. I fall onto my bed. Scarlett starts undressing me and then everything goes black.

I wake up to the sun beaming through my bedroom window, which is typical for a summer morning in California. The heat in my room is unbearable. Why didn't Scarlett close my curtains and open my window last night? My head feels like a high school drum line. I climb out of my bed and go to the bathroom to grab some painkillers and a glass of water. I need this hangover to be gone, like now.

I try to focus on the clock to see what time it is, but my body is still pumping the SoCo and lemonade around my body. Its eleven forty-five. Have I really slept that long? For Scarlett just to leave me here isn't like her at all. I must have really pissed her off last night.

I look around my bedroom for my phone. I see my jeans and blazer on the chair in the corner of my room. I find my phone in the back pocket of my jeans. I see that I have had three texts from Cassidy and two missed calls. Great, she is in panic mode now because I haven't contacted her back. Typical Cassidy.

Me: Hey Cass, I'm fine, really hung-over. text u l8ter ok

I must have slept the day away, as Scarlett wakes me up when she gets in from work. I have to do some grovelling with my big sis to try and get back in her good books.

"Hey Scar, how was work? Are you hungry? I can make us something." It's like I'm begging for her forgiveness, but I only got drunk. It's not like I did something awful, right?

15

Scarlett sits at the dining table while I dish out the take-out she brought home with her. I'm very glad for it, as I'm still in no state to cook for us. We make small talk and Scarlett goes through her plans for her big three-0 party.

"Are you bringing anyone to my party, Tally? I need to know so I can add a plus one." Scarlett looks at me, searching for any clues to see if I have a man in my life, which of course I don't.

"Nope. Sorry Scar, just me." I shrug. I clear our plates away into the sink. My phone rings, but Scarlett gets to it before me. She sees the caller and gives me a full Scarlett Slone smile while handing me the phone.

Without looking at the screen, I answer the call. "Hello?"

"Am I speaking to Natalia Slone?" A man's smooth voice comes through the phone. I look at Scarlett and have a quick glance at my phone screen. Only then do I see the caller Id. The man is calling from Exposure.

"Yes, this is she."

"Oh good. Miss Slone, my name is Tanner and I work at Exposure. We were hoping that we could move your interview to tomorrow at two-fifteen if that is okay with you. Saturday has become unavailable." I look at my sister, who is leaning her elbows on the table, staring at me.

"Yes, of course that will be fine. I can rearrange my work hours." I look at Scarlett who is nodding eagerly, having no clue as to what she is agreeing to. The man lets out a big sigh and I know that he is relieved that I can make the new appointment.

"Oh Miss Slone, you just saved me a whole lot of hassle, thank you. We look forward to seeing you tomorrow at two-fifteen. Have a good evening." I hang up and look at Scarlett. I know I'm blushing big time. My nerves kick in and I begin to shake.

"I need a few hours off tomorrow Scar. They have moved my interview up to tomorrow at two-fifteen." Scarlett jumps around the table and hugs me in a big sis way.

"Ring mom and dad. They are going to want to know." I grip my phone and ring my parents to inform them of the change to my big interview.

After a big talk with my parents, I go upstairs and run a hot bubble bath to help me relax. I lay in the tub, smoothing the bubbles over my silky soft skin and started to get turned on by my thoughts of the hot guy from the bar. What was his name again, something Wilde?

It's funny how I only remember his last name. I chuckle to myself. It's been so long since I last had sex. I let my hands slowly move over my nipples and they harden from my touch. I stop in my tracks and I remember Dean.

My whole body shivers as his face flashes through my head. I shake it off and climb out of the bath. I dry quickly, get into my PJs, and jump into my bed. I lie in bed, staring at the plain white ceiling while 'The Script' plays softly from my iPod. It isn't long until I drift off to sleep.

I wake with a jolt as my alarm stars beeping from my bedside table. I hit the off button and lay there thinking about how I can make this day be over with already. I join Scarlett in the kitchen. "Wow! You're showered and dressed already, you feeling okay?"

She winks at me and I give her a-you-really-have-to-ask look. She turns away, continuing to make our breakfast. I sit in silence to eat my bagel and scrambled egg while Scarlett talks on the phone to someone I'm assuming has something to do with her party.

We drive to work with Iron and Wine's 'Flightless Bird' playing in the car soothing my nerves. When we arrive at work I decide to sort the new stock out which will take my mind off my afternoon appointment. I sort through the new dresses and shoes that have just arrived. It takes most of the day to account all the stock and sort orders, for which I am very grateful.

Scarlett comes into the back office. "Pup it's time to go, you ready?"

I hated her calling me 'Pup', but it's been her and my older brother Jake's nickname for me since I was a baby. They asked our parents for a puppy, but they brought me home instead and the nickname just stuck with me. I look up at Scarlett and I know that the entire color has drained from my face. I take a deep breath and stand.

"Ok, let me just grab my bag." I'm so glad that Scarlett is driving me to Exposure. I don't think I would have been able to drive with my nerves. We arrive at one-fifty-five and Scarlett drops me off outside the rather large white building. She kisses me on the cheek and wishes me good luck before driving off.

I'm on my own looking at this immaculate building.

I'm so glad that I decided to wear my black skirt which stops just above my knees and a cream short sleeve blouse and my flats. 'You got this Tally' I breathe. My phone peeps and I take it out of my bag to check. There are a few texts from family and friends wishing me good luck on my interview.

I walk into the reception area which has a black semi-circle desk that comes right up to chest height with the company name Exposure in bold silver letters. There are doors either side going all the way back which I'm assuming are studios. Just behind the desk are two stair cases, which meet at the top. Everything is white with splashes of silver and black. The receptionist stands when I approach the desk.

"Hi, Natalia Slone for an interview at two-fifteen. I know I'm early" I just look at this perfect looking twenty-something young woman with a perfect face, body and short blond hair. She picks up the phone, hits a number and informs the person on the other end that I've arrived.

"Please take a seat, someone will be with you shortly." I nod and take a seat. I sit and watch as beautiful people come and go. Models, most definitely models. I think to myself that Lucas would be in heaven if he were with me. Not too long after I arrive, a young man maybe early to mid-twenties walks over to the reception desk, glances at me and walks in my direction, stopping just a few feet in front of me.

"Natalia Slone?" Comes a smooth voice from my left.

I stand "Yes?"

"Come with me please." I follow this rather good looking man, all bleached blond hair, blue eyes and tall; he obviously works out. He has to work out to get an ass like that.

He takes me up the stairs and into a large office, where he sits next to Mrs. Silver and another man casually dressed in dark jeans and a tight black t-shirt. Mrs. Silver gives me a look as if she is thinking where she has seen me before.

The blond tells me to sit and I comply. They leave me sitting there while they flick through my portfolio, surely they should have done this before I came in. The blond looks at me and then back to Mrs. Silver. Mr. Casual looks up at me.

"Have you been taking photographs for long Miss Slone?" He asks. I look at them, thinking that I went through all of this when they phoned me the first time.

"I have been taking photos since I was ten years old. My brother Jake bought me a camera for my tenth birthday. It's always been just a hobby for me." They confer amongst themselves. They all turn to me and smile with little giggles.

"Natalia, can I ask a quick question?" I nod yes. "Are you related to Jake Slone of LA Galaxy?"

I smile at the blond hottie. "Yes, Jake is my big brother." He nods and gives me a beautiful smile.

They laugh and Mrs. Silver sits forward in her chair. "This is all for show Natalia, or should I call you Tally. We try to look mean, but we can never keep a straight face," says Mrs. Silver. So, she does remember me. They all relax and come and sit at my end of the table.

"So, who taught you to take such amazing photos, Natalia?" Mr. Casual asks, then realizes that I don't know his name. "Sorry for not introducing myself. I'm Carlos. I'm the head photographer here and I think we are going to get along nicely. I love raw, natural talent like yourself," he says matter of factly.

"Oh, please call me Tally." He nods at me. The hot blond offers me his hand

"I'm Tanner, nice to meet you. I'm the guy who phoned last night." I visibly relax, with the introductions out of the way. We chat for about one hour. Mrs. Silver asks me if I would like Carlos to show me around to see if I like the place, and I agree. I would love to see what goes on inside these big famous studios of Exposure, just in case it will be my last chance. I follow Carlos out of the big room and he starts showing me all the different studios.

Each studio has a different purpose, like the glamour shoots, the family shoots etc. He shows me the aptly named 'E' room, which is where the clients relax before a shoot, where the buffet table is always full and the drinks table looks as if it should belong at a house party,. Even though the whole building looks very professional, it's also very laid back.

Carlos introduces me to staff members as we walk through the different studios and everyone seems really nice and down to earth. As we are walking past one of the back studios, a small group of men walk out in front of us and head for the stairs. Carlos shouts to one of the men and they all stop and turn to face us.

"Hey Sam, this is Tally. She has a job interview here today. I was just showing her around." Not all of the men turn around until I speak.

"Nice to meet you Sam, I have seen some of your photos online. You're amazing." I say to Sam, who is just beautiful. He is a tall, tanned man with jet black hair, green eyes, olive skin, and is very well dressed. The last of the men turns to face us and I go blood red.

Oh my God, it's him.

It's James Wilde!

Chapter 3

James is wearing black jeans with a grey long sleeved Henley and grey vest. So damn hot. I'm locked in a gaze with Wilde. Carlos looks back and forth between Wilde and I.

"Have you guys finished your meeting?" Carlos turns and asks Sam, to which he nods. Wilde is staring right at me as if I'm the only person in the hallway. The men's voices fade into the background. I can't look away from Wilde, our eyes still locked on each other. I can feel my skin heating up. He completely ignores everyone who is talking and comes straight at me. He stops directly in front of me and I can feel his feather light touch on my hip.

"Hello again Tally. Did you enjoy drinks with your friends the other night?" I blush and try to remember my drunken antics.

"I did, thank you. Did you enjoy your evening?" He gives a sexy smirk and I flush again.

"I did also, thank you. I spent most of my night just dancing and enjoying the view." Wilde winks at me. Oh God, what did I do? No he couldn't mean me, could he? I give Carlos a look. He smiles and politely excuses us from the group. I glance back at the men and Wilde is watching me walk away with a very smug look on his face. As we hit the bottom of the stairs, Carlos stops me.

"Do you know James Wilde?" I shake my head and explain.

"He jumped the line at a bar I was at the other night." Carlos and I join Mrs. Silver and Tanner at the reception desk.

They inform me that they have a few more candidates to look at and they will be in touch. I say my goodbyes and make my way out onto the street.

It's a beautiful day yet again, so I stroll back to Scarlett Avenue. It doesn't take long to get there. As I walk through the door, Scarlett comes darting towards me. Thank heavens she can run in heels. She gives me a big sis hug and can't wait to get all the details.

"So? How did it go? They loved you, didn't they?" She asks, a huge smile painted on her face. I'm stunned by her confidence in me.

"They are going to let me know once they finishing interviewing everyone else. It was really nice there, the workers are really friendly and I could be friends with the manager, Carlos. Oh, and Tanner, Mrs. Silver's PA, is very cute." I need to go and give Cassidy the run down on my interview and tell her about my little run in with James 'hot and sexy' Wilde.

At the end of the day, we lock the store up and head to our parents' house for our family night. Mom started this family tradition when we all moved out into our own places. We arrive at our parents' place and mom is in the kitchen with Marcy, her housekeeper, adding the finishing touches to our family meal.

My dad was in his study as always, finishing his lawyer work for the day. I poke my head around his office door and wave. He looks up, giving me a smile and a little wave. Scarlett and I go and say hi to our mom.

"Hey, Mom." I lean in and kiss her on her cheek. "What are you cooking?" My mom signals us to sit at the table in the dining room while she chews on a chunk of food. I'm so happy to see my big brother sitting at the table, tapping away on his laptop. I lean against the door frame.

"Hey hot stuff." I always call him that because that's what my friends called him. They all had a crush on him in high school. Ellie still has a crush on him.

Jake looks up and sees me. He shoots me a big boyish grin, shuts his laptop, and makes his way over to me. Jake is tall like Scarlett, with short brown hair and green eyes. He has one arm covered in a tattooed sleeve. On his wrist is a special tattoo. Jake has a heart with wings on either side. That tattoo symbolises the three of us. He got it after the Dean incident.

"Hey pup, how was the interview?" Jake asks while pulling me in for a hug.

Again with the nickname. I roll my eyes at him. He gives me a big bear hug and almost squeezes all the air from my lungs.

"Oh God Jake, I can't breathe. Put me down you ape," I say, breathless. Jake puts me down, not letting go of my hands, and twists my ring on my finger. He has done that since he and Scarlett gave it to me. We haven't seen each other in a few weeks because he was on tour with his soccer team. Jake has played soccer for LA Galaxy for two years now. He plays left wing and is awesome, if I do say so myself. I'm very proud of my big brother.

He gives Scarlett a big hug and we all sit at the table and chat while waiting for our parents come to join us. After our parents join us, we start eating our meal.

Marcy has done amazing yet again, with roast chicken, potatoes, and the typical vegetables. I have known Marcy all my life. She is like another member of our family. I'm driving, so Scarlett is having a glass of wine or two. The conversation is about how my dad's day went, even though he couldn't go into full details of his case. We also chatted about my interview.

My dad is good looking for his age. He is an older looking version of Jeffery Dean Morgan. "How did the interview go Natalia?" My dad turns to me and asks, so I go into full detail about how it went. I tell them how amazing Mrs Silver is, how Carlos would be great to work for, and that I could really enjoy working there.

I didn't say anything about James Wilde being there. My body temperature raises just thinking about him and a slight throb starts between my legs.

Why does he have this effect on me??

After we have finished eating, my dad and Jake go and watch soccer on TV while Scarlett, my mom, and I take to the kitchen and have a nice girly chat about clothes, shoes, handbags and Scarlett's birthday party of course. She is having a big, lavish, cocktail style party. Ladies will be in evening gowns and the men in tuxes. I'm so not looking forward to wearing an evening gown and heels. I don't do heels and Scarlett knows this, but she says I have to, as it's her big three-0 birthday.

As the night winds down, we say our goodbyes to our parents and the three of us leave. I'm glad I'm driving, as Scarlett drank a little more than a one or two glasses of wine. We have to drop Jake off at his place, as it's on our way home anyway.

I'm driving and we are all singing at the top of our voices to 'Lazy Song' by Bruno Mars. Scarlett and Jake are going crazy doing the dance moves, but it's so nice to be here with my big sister and brother. I love them to death.

I pull up outside Jake's apartment building, which is very modern looking, but he can afford it on his salary. Even though it should be the big brother taking care of me, I watch him enter the building before I pull away. Scarlett is still singing as loud as she can beside me, while waving at our brother.

We arrive at our house and I pull the car onto the drive. Scarlett climbs out and walks, well stumbles into the house while I get both our bags and fish for the keys out of my bag, which is like a Mary Poppins bag. I can't find a damn thing in it.

After such a hectic day I'm beat, so as soon as I put Scarlett to bed, I head to my room. I throw my bag and jacket onto a chair in the corner of my room. I get into my bed shorts and vest and climb into bed, knowing that there is nothing more I can do about Exposure.

Staring at my curtains, as they gently float with the gentle breeze coming through my bedroom window, I slip into a deep sleep. I start to dream of sexy smiles with beautiful ocean-blue eyes until my alarm goes off. I turn it off and stretch out. I'm feeling quite refreshed from my deep sleep. My body obviously needed it. I trek to the bathroom, do my usual morning routine and head back into my room to get dressed for work.

Since Scarlett let me have a few hours off for my interview, I offered to work the next morning. Saturday's the busiest day of the week for the store.

All staff was in and having a blast, music playing. Customers are enjoying the music and the register was filling up, so all in all, it's a pretty good day. Scarlett is in a very good mood since she didn't have a hangover this morning. She gave me her credit card to go out and pick up lunch for all the staff at our usual deli. As I stroll down the street enjoying the sun on my face, watching people going about their Saturday lunch time, spending their well-earned cash, I hear my name being called from across the street.

I stop and raise my hand to shade my eyes from the sun even though I'm wearing sun glasses. Focusing across the street, I see this Sex God like figure cross the street with ease, stopping cars as he crossed each lane. He is tall, his light brown hair slightly brushed to one side.

My breath hitches when I notice who it is that's calling my name. He is wearing a tight, red, V-neck t-shirt, which just hugs all his sculptured body, hip hanging Levis, and white Converse. Wow, he looks stunning. He stops right in front of me and looks straight into my eyes. I could get totally lost in those beautiful blue eyes.

"Hey," James says and waits for my response.

"Hi," is just about all I can manage. He just looks so hot. I struggle to take him all in.

"How was the interview at Exposure? They are a great bunch of people, you will enjoy working with them. They know how to treat their clients," He says with a huge grin on his face, as if he is speaking from experience.

I look up at him. I can feel my face change color and my body temperature rise, but I answer him as calmly as I can.

"It went great, thank you. I think I would enjoying working with Carlos, Sam and a few of the others." I add, "Mrs Silver seems like a lovable lady to work for." Wilde looks at me and I get the sense that he is undressing me with his eyes. I'm wearing a green summer dress that comes mid-thigh with flats that Scarlett made me wear. I'm glad she did now.

"Cool, so where are you going now?" James asks. Why is he interested? I point down the street.

"Going to the deli to get Subs for everyone back at the store." Do I want to walk away from him, or shall I invite him for the short walk just so that I can keep talking and looking at him. "If you've got no plans at this moment in time, would you like to join me for the walk down?" James looks quite happy with my request. He nods and gestures for me to lead the way. "So, how is the show coming?" I ask.

Wilde gives me a quizzed look.

"You don't watch a lot of TV, do you?" I shake my head. It's true, I don't. I would rather take photos, read a book, or just listen to music. I have never been much a TV person, even as a child. I watch some with Scarlett and we have our favorite shows, but not too many.

"I am on a break between filming at the moment. I have just finished filming season two, so we are in editing at the moment."

"Cool." What else was there to say? Wilde laughs and we carry on walking.

"Have you always been into photography?" Wilde asks me.

"Since I was ten. My brother Jake bought me my first camera and it just took off as my favorite hobby."

I look up at him and he is smiling at me. "Have you always been into acting?" He shrugs.

"Kind of. I wanted to be a soccer player when I was younger, but didn't give it my all. I was spotted by a modelling agency in my teens and I did that for a few years until the audition came up for a show a few years back. I stayed there for a two seasons, but then I was asked to come on board for 'Control' and well, the rest is history."

As we approach the deli, Wilde looks at me and out of the blue asks, "Maybe I can take you to the movies one night, maybe dinner too?" He runs the back of his hand down my arm and my body shivers. Wilde smiles because he can see the effect he has on me. "Would you be okay with that?" I'm in shock as to why James Wilde would ask me out on a date. He is wanted by so many women, he could have anyone he desires. Why on Earth is he asking me?

"What makes you think that I don't already have a boyfriend?" I smirk at him.

"Do you?" He looks at me with what I can only say is as slightly annoyed expression on his face. "I asked you a question Tally, are you going to put me out of my misery?" Wilde just keeps glaring at me like I actually owe him an answer.

"Why are you looking at me like that?" I frown at him.

He shrugs "I want to know if you have a boyfriend or not, but since you're stalling, I'm inclined to say that you don't."

"I'm not stalling. I barely know you and you're asking about my relationship status." He steps closer to me.

"Well I think I have a right to know, don't you? If I'm going to take you out, I should know. Is the dude from the bar the other night your boyfriend?" I know I have a confused look on my face, but James either doesn't see it or ignores it.

"What dude?" He smirks and shakes his head.

"You were sitting with him and he kissed you. I have a right to know Tally." I shake my head in complete disbelief.

"You're an ass, you know that?" I go to walk off, but I feel his hand grip my elbow.

"I'm sorry Tally." Wilde's eyes soften, but it's too late. I'm not taking crap from guys anymore. I pull my arm away, walk to the deli door and turn back to Wilde.

"Good Bye James." I turn and head into the deli. I stand in the order line, my heart beating fast. I turn to look out the window and see James still standing there with a pained look on his face. Why is he still here? He takes his phone out of his pocket and starts talking.

He looks up from the sidewalk and our eyes lock again. I turn and look back at the counter.

Chapter 4

That evening, I stay at home with myself and a bubble bath for company. Scarlett and her friends have gone out to one of Scarlett's friend's engagement party. I lay in my bath, blowing the bubbles off my hands, the music is playing softly from my iPod. I lay back and relax; it's so soothing, just me, the bubbles, and the music.

My bliss is disrupted by my phone ringing playing DJ Fresh ft Rita Ora's Hot Right Now as my ringtone. I dry my hand with a nearby hand towel and reach for my phone; I have to stretch, as it's on the unit, out of waters way. I can't reach, so I struggle to reach over and manage to reach my phone, wondering whose stupid ass idea was it put my phone out of reach.

"Hello?" As I answer, my hand slips off the side of the bath and I hit the cold floor with a thud.

Ouch, fuck that hurt.

"Tally are you there? Tally, are you OK? For fuck sake, answer me Tally, please?" That's what I hear from my phone, which by some miracle is still in my hand. I put the phone to my ear, still on my bathroom floor butt naked and answer.

"Hey, sorry. I had a bit of an accident, but I'm fine … I think." Pulling myself into the sitting position and leaning against the bath, I pull a towel down onto my now hurting body.

"Tally, I'm coming over. You may need to go to the ER. DON'T MOVE OK?" He sounded very adamant. I didn't get time to answer, as he hung up before I could say anything. I struggle to my feet and make my way to my room.

I remove my towel and check my body for any bruises. I have a lump on my head from it hitting the floor. My left shoulder is aching and my hip and wrist are hurting, but everything else seems fine. I go to my closet, throw a vest and bed shorts on, and start brushing my hair. I'm looking at myself in the mirror. Now that I think about it, who was that voice on the other end of that phone? I grab my phone and check caller ID, but it's a number that I don't know.

Do I call him back, or just wait? It must be someone I know because he called me Tally and has my number. After drying my hair, I sit on my bed rubbing my shoulder, when there is a sudden knock on my front door and the door opens. I hear footsteps, but I'm too dazed to go and take a look at who it is. I must know them. I hear the same urgent phone voice calling my name.

"Tally! Tally where are you?" He shouts. He startles me, but I recognize the voice.

It's James Wilde.

"I'm up here, come up." I hear him run up the stairs and stride past my room, but comes back when he sees me sitting crossed legged on my bed.

Why is he here? How did he get my number?

Wilde enters my room and sits on my bed, so close that his knee is touching mine. "Are you okay? What the fuck happened? I phoned you, you answered, then I heard a massive bang. You went all quiet. Are you hurt anywhere?" His eyes scan my body for any signs of injury.

"I'm fine. I was reaching for my phone and I slipped out of the bath." I looked down at my wrist and gently rub. Suddenly, Wilde's hand is pulling my wrist towards him. He starts smoothing my wrist, leaving trails of heat over my skin from his touch.

"Does it hurt that bad? Do you think it's broken?" I shake my head; it's not broken, but sore from the fall. I snatch my wrist back and look at Wilde right in the eyes.

"Why were you phoning me? How did you get my number?" James smiles. *If he can make me feel like this just by looking at me, God help me if actually touches me the way I so want him to. Ok where did that come from?*

"Blame your sister, she was at the same party as me. I saw you walk out of her store the other day, so I went over and quizzed her about you. Little did I know that you're the baby sister of the owner of Scarlett Avenue. We got talking about you and I asked her for your number. She was more than willing to give it up to me, but she threatened me not to hurt you." James smiles.

"Plus, I wanted to apologize for what happened this afternoon." What the hell was Scarlett playing at, meddling in my social life? I don't have a love life, not since Dean.

I shudder at the thought of him. Scarlett was always looking out for me in all aspects of my life, but she needs to butt out of this department. I'm twenty-four years old and can handle myself. She has been even more protective since Dean. Scarlett blames herself in a small way. She felt that she let me down, even after all the times I told her she was not to blame for anything that he did to me.

I can't help but wonder why James Wilde is sitting here on my bed with me when he should be out clubbing and picking up some airhead who only wants to have sex with him. Okay, I want to have to sex with him, but that's not the point.

"James, I think you can go now. I'm fine. Thank you for checking up on me, but you can go back to whatever you were doing." I wave my hand around.

He ignores me. I climb off my bed in a gesture for him to leave but things don't go my way. As I stand, I lose my balance as a result of banging my head from my earlier bathroom fall. James catches me and places me back onto my bed.

"Sit." I push his hands off of me. He holds his hands up in defence. "Sorry for trying to help and not letting you fall over and crack your head, again!" He has annoyance in his voice with a hint of sarcasm. He stands, leaning against the door frame. He crosses his big arms across his chest, crosses his legs at his ankles and stares at me.

"I'm fine. I don't need you here, please just go" *Oh God, my head is banging.* I rub my temples.

"Do you really want me to go and leave you here alone when you're feeling like this?" I nod without looking at him. Wilde shakes his head and rolls his eyes. By the look on Wilde's face, he isn't used to girls asking him to leave their bedrooms. "I'm not leaving you Tally, you could have a concussion." I'm praying I keep my balance as I stand.

"Listen I'm fine now, just go back to the party and pick up some Barbie wannabe and forget about me, okay?" He turns and starts to walks out of my room, still shaking his head. He stops in the doorway.

"Maybe I don't want to forget about you." He exits my room.

My heart sinks, but I'm confused as to why I'm feeling like this. I hear the front door open and then close; I walk over to my bedroom window and watch James walk towards a black BMW M6 Convertible. *Wow, now that is a sexy car.* As James opens the door, he looks back at the house and then up to my window. He shakes his head, climbs in his car, and speeds away.

I close my curtains and climb back into my bed. I pull the blanket over me and drift off to sleep. Not sure how much time has passed, but I wake to the front door being slammed shut, indicating that my sister is home. I'm still dazed from my fall in the bathroom, but I shake it off. I head downstairs, dreading what state I'm going to find Scarlett in. As I walk down the stairs, I can hear my big sister cursing and it's kind of funny.

"Shit, fuck. Who the fuck put that table there?" Scarlett stumbles into the kitchen and bumps into everything in sight. I enter the kitchen to find my big sister raiding the fridge for munchies. God, is she drunk. She turns and looks at me with a carrot stick hanging out of her mouth.

"Hey Pup, whatcha doing? I am starving and there's not any food in the fridge." She pouts and points at the fridge, but I know very well that the fridge is full of food. I look at the clock on the kitchen wall and its one thirty am. Thank the heavens we don't open Scarlett Avenue on a Sunday. Scarlett is going to have a hangover tomorrow. Serves her right.

"Do you want to me run out and grab you something to eat?" Scarlett nods with a huge greedy grin on her face. I go back up to my room and throw a pair of jeans, a hoodie, and my Converse and head back downstairs. I ignore my drunken sister in the kitchen. Whatever mess she has made, she can clean it up tomorrow.

I jump into my Jeep and reverse out of the drive. I head down to Scarlett's favorite burger. Rossi's is a high end burger place; only the upper class eat there. It's full of rich kids and packed with people who are ending their night of partying. Everyone is dressed to the nines and I'm in jeans and a hoodie. *Oh well.*

I head to the counter, place Scarlett's order, take a seat, and wait to be called, while playing on my phone. I'm sitting at a small, round metallic table, watching everyone come and go. Some people are eating in. I watch a couple in the corner who are all mouth and hands; I think he wants to eat her, not the burger on the table in front of him.

I stare at this couple, feeling like a voyeur, when they suddenly stop kissing and the guy looks up at me. I blush a whole new color of red. He winks at me with a very hot smile on his face and I can't help but smile back at him. He goes back to kissing the girl.

"Order for Tally Slone." Oh, a welcome distraction from the couple making out in the corner. I collect my order and turn back towards the door when a girl steps out in front of me and gives me the once over with her eyes.

"Oh excuse me, can I pass please?" She doesn't move, she just gives a like-I-give-a-fuck look. I have no idea who she is by the way.

"So you're Tally Slone?" I look at her with a puzzled look on my face.

"Yes. Do I know you?" I have no freaking idea who this chick is. She doesn't reply instantly, she looks me up and down again.

"I'm Carly, Dean's new girlfriend." She informs me looking rather pleased with herself. I'm utterly shocked by her. What I ever done to her?

"Ok well good for you. Now move please, my food is getting cold." I try to step around her, but she steps with me. "Right, what is your problem exactly?" Again she doesn't reply straight away. It's like she has to think of a comeback.

"I don't like bitches like you going around spreading nasty ass rumours about my boyfriend. You don't have any proof to back your shady story up." I look at her wide eyed. *Oh so this is where this is going.*

"Really? You don't know jack shit about Dean and my situation okay? Now please move." I notice out of the corner of my eye that everyone has stopped eating and talking and are watching us, maybe to see who throws the first punch maybe? Well it most certainly isn't going to be me.

"Dean has told me everything about you two, how he loved you will all his heart and you ruined him by making that story up". I can't believe that Dean would tell her everything and lied about what happened between us.

Dean never loved me, he wanted a toy that he could do whatever he pleased with. It wasn't even about the money because Dean came from money, his dad was a big time finance guy and his mom was a trophy wife. The whole burger joint is still silent. Carly and I are just looking at each other when the bell above the door rings to signal that someone has entered the restaurant. I take a look at a group of girls sitting on the table to my left; they are smiling and giggling at whoever just entered through the door.

I go back to looking Carly, who still hasn't taken her evil eyes off me. If looks could kill, I would be dead and buried by now. I'm locked in her gaze, kind of in fear for my safety. In that moment I feel an arm snake around my waist and a kiss on my temple.

"There you are baby, I was wondering what was keeping you. So, who is your friend?" I'm shocked to see Wilde standing next to me with his hand on my hip.

Carly just stands there staring at Wilde. To be honest, I'm both relieved and confused as to why his arm is around my waist, holding me tight to his body. Not that I'm complaining, this man smells amazing. He looks down at me and hugs me tighter, so I place my arm around his waist, slip my hand under his jacket, and grip a handful of his t-shirt.

"She isn't a friend, just someone who thought she knew me! Let's go." James pulls me towards the door and we exit Rossi's, everyone still stunned that he has been in the same room as them. I'm really surprised that he wasn't mobbed by anyone. James leads me to his car; I stop as he opens the car door.

"I came in my car. I'm fine now, thank you. I can drive myself home. Thanks again, James." I start walking away from him, not looking back. I can't encourage this. James is at my side within seconds.

"I will walk you to your car. It's past two in the morning. I don't like you walking the streets on your own. It isn't safe, Tally." We approach my jeep and James's face falls. I don't think he likes my jeep.

I drive a Jeep Wrangler in white and she is all mine. I love her. "You drive that? Is this a joke, babe?"

I shake my head. What does he have against my Wrangler? Hang on, did Wilde just call me babe?

"Just because I have money, doesn't mean I should flash it, James. She is perfect for me, gets me from A to B safely." James looks at me amused.

"She?"

"Yes she, you got a problem with that as well?" I snap back as I place our food onto the passenger seat. James holds his hands up and walks around my Wrangler. Again James is standing in front of me and he smells delicious, as he has the other times he has been within touching distance.

"Does she have a name too?" I look up at him and shake my head. He has the most beautiful eyes I have ever seen. James touches a strand of my hair and rubs it between his fingers. "You have beautiful hair, Natalia."

He runs the back of his fingers down my cheek. "And such soft skin." I blush, as no man has ever spoken to me like this before. He runs his thumb along my bottom lip. My body comes alive; a prickly wave runs through me. He stares right into my eyes and lifts my chin.

"Can I kiss you, Tally?"

Before I can answer, James Wilde's soft lips are on mine. He licks my bottom lip, so I open my mouth and his tongue plays with mine in my mouth. Oh my God. Wilde tastes of beer and rich chocolate. Something he's had at the party maybe? His hand is at the nape of my neck, holding me close to him. James's kisses are turning me on. I want to touch him. I place my hand on his forearms. I'm enjoying the moment. I lose myself in the kiss, which I haven't been done for so long, but I get snapped back to reality.

I hear Carly the Freak's voice. An image of Dean flashes through my head and I pull back from James. Shocked and shaken, I look at James, who looks confused.

"I'm sorry James, but I can't do this. I'm sorry."

I jump into my Wrangler and pull away, leaving Wilde standing on the sidewalk. I drive back to my place with tears streaming down my face. Dean has ruined any chance of me having a normal relationship with anyone. I hate him for what he did to me.

Chapter 5

The next morning I clean up after Scarlett, as she is no fit state to be doing anything. She is crashed on the sofa, barking orders at me. The cleaning is all done and I sit on the opposite end of the sofa with Scarlett's feet resting on my legs. We curl up and watch re-runs of Supernatural, our all-time favourite TV show. C'mon, who doesn't love a bit of Jesnen Ackles and Jared Padalecki? I think they are the only reason I watch TV. Yum

In the afternoon, Cassidy pops around for a visit and we sit in my room having a girly chat about anything and everything. I love chatting to Cassidy. She never saw me as the girl with the millionaire family. She saw me for me. We shared everything except boys, now anyway. Cassidy has been my rock through my hard times with Dean. We sit on my bed talking about my job interview. "So did you meet any hot guys at the interview?" She shoots me a wicked smile.

"Well, Carlos is hot very hot, but gay. Tanner is cute though." Tanner is kind of cute. He's a few years older than me I think. I stare down at my knotted hands. "I bumped into James Wilde again. He was there having a meeting about an upcoming shoot." Cassidy's eyes shoot open in surprise and she becomes speechless. This is very unlike Miss Cassidy Blake.

She finally speaks after a few moments. "And? Did he see you? Did he speak to you? Come on Tally, I want to know everything." I tell Cassidy about the run in and then of course I have to tell her about the kiss.

"That's not the only time I have seen him, Cass." I explain about him phoning me, me falling out of the bath, and the run in with The Freak.

"He walked me to my car. He told me I had nice hair and soft skin." Cassidy was at a loss for words, yet again. Even though Cassidy and me have done a lot of things together, I still blush telling her all this. "Say something Cass, please?" She shakes her head.

"Oh my God! Tally, James Wilde likes you. I mean, girl, he really likes you! Did he kiss you?"

I blush all kinds of red and Cassidy jumps off of my bed and squeals like a teenage girl. "I knew it. I could tell by the way he looked at you that night in JAG. Are you seeing him again? Natalia Grace Slone, you have to see him again!" I looked back down at my hands and Cassidy knew.

Cassidy looked more gutted than me, but I wasn't ready for a new relationship yet. We chatted most of the evening, talking about how things were with her boyfriend, Josh, and what I had to wear when I went to work. Around nine o'clock, we decided to call it a night. We both had work the next morning.

Scarlett's Avenue was quiet this Monday morning, so I checked the stock. Scarlett was on the phone, leaning on the counter, arranging everything for her party, which was fast approaching. She was very adamant about how she wants things to look. Scarlett has booked a big Dj and an artist to perform at the party, but I know she isn't going to let on who it is.

I'm sitting on the stool behind the counter next to my sister, when my phone starts to ring. I dig it out of the back pocket of my shorts. I look at the caller Id and my heart goes into overdrive. I give Scarlett a quick glance and she frowns as she looks at me. Scarlett ends her call and pushes for me to answer my phone.

"Hello?" A familiar voice came through the speaker.

"Good morning Tally, its Mrs. Silver from Exposure. How are you this fine Monday morning?" I look at Scarlett, who is leaning right into me, trying to hear who was on the other end of the call.

"Good Morning Mrs. Silver. I'm very well, thank you. How are you?" Scarlett's eyes widen and a huge smile spreads across her flawless face.

"I'm good, thank you for asking. Well Tally, I was calling you this morning to offer you the job. I was really hoping that you accept and come down to the studio sometime today or tomorrow so we can go over all the details for you to start." With wide eyes, I look at Scarlett.

A big smile creeps across my face and my big sister knows exactly what has just happened. She starts jumping around the store. I try to stifle my laugh by biting down on my bottom lip, but it doesn't work very well.

"Oh my God, Mrs. Silver, are you sure? I mean umm yes of course yes. I would love to come and work for you, oh my. Wow. Thank you so much. Um, would tomorrow be ok, as I am working today?" Mrs Silver gives me the time to pop around to Exposure and go through all my work details.

I'm in shock. Scarlett and I are dancing around the store like a pair of kindergarten children. I have to phone my parents and Cassidy. I know that Cassidy will inform all my friends.

Scarlett stops dancing and says, "We have to go out and celebrate."

My alarm wakes me at six am. It's my first day as an Exposure and I want to be up and ready. It's been just four days since I was offered the job and I haven't been sleeping that much since. I have been nervous about this very day. Scarlett is in the kitchen. I come down stairs all dressed and ready to go.

I am wearing pale blue skinny jeans, a black Exposure t-shirt, and my black flats. The t-shirt is a little too tight for my liking, but it's uniform. I don't wear a lot of make-up, but today Scarlett told me to wear just a little. I walk into the reception area and the receptionist greets me.

"Good morning, Natalia." I smile politely and return the greeting.

"Good morning, please call me Tally. I don't know your name." She cocks her heard to one side.

"You're new, so it will take some time for you to learn everyone's names. Hi, I'm Isabella, but my friends call me Bella." I smile at her and know that we are going to be good friends. She has that down to earth vibe about her.

"Well I'm hoping that I will get to call you Bella. I'll catch you later." I smile and walk around the desk and up the stairs. Sam meets me the top and kisses me on both cheeks.

"Morning Miss Tally, I hope you're ready to get started. We have a fun family week, lots of screaming children and bitchy mothers who want the perfect family picture." I can't help but giggle at his comment. We walk down the corridor past a few of the studios that Carlos showed me on the day of my interview.

We stop at Studio Five. Sam looks at me with a big grin on his face.

"You ready?" I nod and he pushes the door open and hushes me into the room.

"This is all yours, Tally."

The studio is fantastic, all white walls with three windows; it has all the equipment that an everyday photographer needs.

"Is this really all mine?" I turn to look at Sam; he nods with a big smile on his face.

"I will leave you to your studio." He kisses my cheek. "Welcome to Exposure, Natalia." Sam leaves the studio. I wonder around my studio, getting familiar with all the equipment. The hair and make-up stations are all neat and tidy, all the costumes are hanging perfectly. Just the way I like things.

My studio phone rings and I walk over to my desk and answer, "Hello?"

"Tally, it's Bella. Your ten o'clock is here. Shall I send them up to your studio?"

"Um, I have a booking this morning? I didn't know." There a small pause from Bella.

"Tally on the desk next to the phone you will find a clipboard with a list of you clients for the week, okay?" Panic starts to rise in my head. "I will send your clients up to you now." With that, Bella hangs up. I look around my studio. I can feel the color creep over my body. I hear shouting children running in the hallway.

God help me!

My first week goes pretty fast. Sam was right, lots of screaming children and very bitchy moms, but it wasn't just one day, it was a whole week of it. Every night I went home with a headache and every night I would just jump straight into bed. It's Friday. I'm cleaning my desk and I glance at the clock. It's six fifteen. Carlos comes into my studio.

"Hey Tally, how's today been? Any better?" I raise an eyebrow at him.

"It's been crazy. I don't think I have stopped all week, let alone all day. Is every week like this?" I have a pleading look on my face now. Carlos smiles at me, put his arm around my shoulder, and pulls me out of my studio.

"Let's get you a strong drink, shall we?" We meet Sam and Tanner, who are at the bottom of the stairs discussing a photo shoot that is coming up.

"Hey Tally, you had a fun week?" Tanner asks. I smile.

"I need a drink, who is buying?" The three hot men all smile and laugh as we exit the studio. We are sitting in a bar with most of the Exposure's staff. Everyone is enjoying the night, chatting about their week about any awkward clients. Sam buys everyone tequila shots as a celebration of my first week as a full time Exposure employee.

We all down our shots, lick our salt, suck our limes, and demand more. Bella and I are dancing with each other. I know we are really going to get along just fine. Cassidy will love her. I feel my head spin slightly and I know that's my cue to stop drinking. I head to the bar and ask for a bottle of water. I turn towards the dance floor and see Bella dancing, when Tanner comes up behind her and starts grinding into her.

She is enjoying it, by the look on her face. Their dancing is sexy and everyone is enjoying the show, not looking surprised by their intimate dancing. I didn't realize they were a couple, but then again maybe they aren't. Carlos stands next to me by the bar and leans back on his elbow on the bar.

"Tanner has had a thing for Bella for some time now. It's nice to finally see him make a move" I smile.

"They look like they need to go home and get rid of some of that bottled up sexual frustration." We burst out laughing and Carlos goes to speak, but stops and looks behind me.

"They won't be the only ones going home for some relieving. Be safe, Tally." Carlos kisses me on the cheek, winks at me, and walks away.

I continue to look at Carlos in a confused manner. What did he mean by that? My body stiffens as I can smell him, then I can feel him. Wilde presses his body flush against mine, my back to his hard front. He places his arm around my waist and holds me there.

"God, you smell good." I stand there, unable to move. James slides my hair to one side and lightly kisses my neck "I have thought of nothing else since our kiss. I want to kiss you more Tally. I can't seem to think of anything or anyone else but you." His grip tightens and my body burns with desire. I turn in his arms to face him, his grip not letting go.

"Why James? I don't get why you like me. Why do you want to kiss me?" He looks into my eyes. The alcohol is making me more confident.

"Why not? God you are so sexy. You have the softest lips I have ever kissed, and I want to kiss them again, and again." He stops, closes his eyes, and when he opens them, I can see that he means what he is saying to me.

"I want to kiss every inch of your body Tally, please let me. I won't hurt you." That threw me. What did he the hell did he mean he won't hurt me?

I pull out of his hold. "What the fuck do you mean you won't hurt me? Have you been talking to Scarlett again?" James looks just as shocked and confused as me.

"Look Tally, I haven't spoken to your sister it's just … the way you reacted when I kissed you the other night, it looked to me that you have had your heart broken before." I'm looking at Wilde and softening towards him when my phone rings. I answer without looking at who it is. I keep my eyes locked on Wilde, he staring right back at me.

Chapter 6

"Hello?" My stomach falls when I hear sobbing on the other end. It's Josh.

"It's Cassidy, oh my God Tally! Cass and I were in an accident tonight. She is at the hospital. I didn't see it until it hit us." The color drained from my face, my legs went weak, and James holds me close to his chest. He takes the phone from my hand. I hear him speak into my phone.

"Okay, I'll get her there." I'm not sure how long I stood there but I was unaware that all my co-workers are now standing around me. James explained to them what has happened. They all hugged me one by one but I couldn't feel anything. I'm completely numb. The next thing I know, I'm sitting in James's car and he has his hand on mine, squeezing lightly. The drive took forever, James weaving through traffic to get me to the hospital as quick as possible.

We arrive at ER and James talks to a nurse at the nurses' station. He pulls me in close and holds me tight, for which I'm grateful, and we walk into the elevator. I look up at James. His eyes are so soft, the way he is looking at me. He runs his thumb over my cheek. "What floor are we going to?" I ask.

"Sixth floor. Cassidy is in the OR already, baby. We will know more when we get up there, okay?" He runs his fingers over my cheek again, soothing me some. I have only now noticed that I'm holding James tight against my own body. I think if either of us let go I'm going to crumble to the floor.

The door opens and James supports me as we walk out. I see Cassidy's mom, Karen. She is rocking in her chair while Cassidy's dad tries to comfort her. Josh is pacing the room.

There are two police officers talking to a nurse. I walk towards the family and Karen looks up. She comes darting towards me with open arms. James tries to step away but I grab the bottom of his shirt.

"Don't leave me." James nods his head and stands by my side once again, holding my hand.

"I'm not going anywhere, baby."

I try to comfort Karen as we both sob on each other shoulders. She finally lets me go and I hug Joe, Cassidy's dad. All the while I'm still holding James's hand. Josh can barely keep still. He has a broken arm and a cut on the left side of his chin. I sit down next to Karen and James sits next to me. I look at Josh and he sits opposite us.

"What happened, Josh?" He looks racked with guilt.

"We were walking back to my car after we saw a gig in one of the clubs." He stops and put his hands on either side of his head. "I didn't see it Tally, I swear." I'm confused.

"See what?" James tightens his grip on my hand, sort of signalling to back off of him and let him speak. Josh continues.

"A cab lost control, mounted the sidewalk, and hit us. Cassidy was on the outside, so she took the full force of the impact." I gasp. How could he have stopped this? He couldn't have.

"Josh, there was no way in hell that you could stop any of this. You do know that right?" He looks lost, but doesn't answer me. Time passes slowly as we wait for news on my best friend, my non-biological sister. I pray in my head for her to be alright. I don't know what I would do if anything was to happen to her.

James has finally left my side and has gone to get everyone a coffee. This is the first time he has left me since we got to the hospital, and I'm so grateful that he has stayed. I think I would have fallen to pieces if he wasn't here with me.

Joe stands and taps Karen on the shoulder as a Dr in blue scrubs walks through the double doors, the same double doors that we have all been staring at the past few hours. They all stand and walk forward.

"Mr. and Mrs. Blake? Hi, I'm Dr. Benson. I operated on Cassidy. She suffered internal bleeding, which we managed to control. Now she did lose a lot of blood, but she should make a full recovery. Everything has been repaired and there shouldn't be any long term damage. She is still sedated, and will be for up to forty-eight hours. You can go and see her in about thirty minutes after we get settle her into her room." Joe and Karen hug and get hold of Josh also.

I fall against the wall and sink to the floor, my legs just buckling underneath me. The tears start to roll down my cheeks and I can't stop crying. James arrives back with everyone's drinks and sees me on the floor.

"Any news?" He lifts my chin up to look at him.

"She's alive, they are keeping her sedated for now. She's alive, James." He smiles at me and I finally let a smile appear on my face.

He places the coffee holder down and sinks to the floor next to me. He places his arm around my shoulders and pulls me in tightly to him, holding me while I sob my heart out again.

Cassidy looks so young in her hospital bed. Even though she is twenty-four, she looks much younger. She is asleep, but breathing on her own, which is a good thing. She has a few grazes on her face, but nothing major, which I know she will be very happy with, no scarring. Joe, Karen, and Josh sit by her side.

"Karen, I will go to Cass's apartment and get a few things for her, okay? Josh, do you want anything?" He shakes his head. He can't speak. He just sits there holding Cassidy's hand.

Joe stands. "Tally, go home sweetie. I will run by Cass's place and get a few things for her and Josh." He says, giving Josh a look. "You look shattered and we will need you to cover for us when we need to rest sweetie, okay?" There is no point in arguing with Joe, so I nod in agreement and hug them both. I give my best friend a kiss on her forehead and leave her room. James and I walk to the elevators and a nurse stops him.

"Hi, are you really the James Wilde from that TV show?" James looks at me and back to the nurse.

"No, sorry you have the wrong guy." He shrugs and pulls me into the elevator. He still hasn't let me go.

"Why didn't you tell her yes? She knew who you were, James" I'm confused as to why he told her no.

"Now isn't the time to be having photos with fans or signing autographs. I'm here for you, not for me." Wow, his reply shocks me. I wouldn't have minded, but I understand now why he told her no.

We arrive in the underground parking and I lean against the car, still trying to take it all in. I can't believe I could have lost my best friend tonight.

So much has happened this week and I just want to curl up and sleep for a week. James comes back around to my side of the car and hooks a strand of hair behind my ear. His soft fingers trace my jaw line. My tired body responds to him.

I place my hand over his. "Thank you for staying with me. I really don't know if I could have coped without you." He gives me a sweet shy smile.

"I'm glad that you let me stay. I want to be here for you Tally, I do. I really like you and if you give me half a chance to show you how I feel about you, you won't regret it." I smile and give him a gentle kiss on the cheek before getting into his car.

The next few days blur into each other. Mrs. Silver had given me as much time off work as I needed, which is great since Cassidy still remained unconscious. The doctor said they would bring her out of the sedation slowly and she will wake when she is ready. All her scans showed no injury to her brain, which is good. It was my time to sit with my best friend while her parents and Josh took some time away from her bedside. It was hard to get Josh to leave her, but he gave in and went home for some sleep.

I came in today on my own. James had a few things to take care of in relation with his TV show. We have been spending most days here together, even though we sit in silence most of the time. I looked through the unit next to Cassidy's hospital bed for her hair brush. She would not be happy if she woke up and saw the state of her hair. While I gently brush my best friend's hair, a young nurse comes into her room, looks at her chart, and then up at us.

"Are you the girl who visits with that really hot actor?" I stop brushing Cassidy's hair and look at the nurse. Where is she going with this?

"Which guy?"

"You know, the actor. James Wilde" She keeps looking at me, but I hold her stare. "So is he your boyfriend? Because I haven't heard anything about him having a girlfriend." I am shocked that she has even come in here while at work to ask me about a visitor.

51

"Aren't you working? I don't think it's very professional to come in here and ask about one of your patient's visitors." She blinks at me and a creepy smile spreads across her face.

"Well, for his sake, I hope that you're not his girlfriend. He could do so much better." I blink at her in utter shock that she has just spoken to me like that. Then I notice something off with her nurse's uniform.

"Hang on, you're not an actual nurse, are you? You don't wear the same color scrubs." I walk to her at the bottom of the bed, stand right in front of her, and we are face to face, as she is short like me. "How dare you come in here and tell me that I'm not good enough for him. You don't know me, or him." She cuts me off.

"Actually I do know him. He is James Wilde from Control. I have been a fan for a while now. He has appeared in a few other TV shows, but this is his first lead role. I know everything there is to know about him. He is a player. He will never settle for a plain thing like you. Wilde only dates high class girls." She says smugly.

"Well honey, I guess that leaves you out of the picture also, huh?" Another nurse walks past the room. "Excuse me?" The forty-something nurse enters Cassidy's room and looks at us.

"Yes? Is everything okay with Miss Blake?"

"Yes Cassidy is fine. I was just wondering what would happen if I was to put in a complaint against an- " I look at this girl and wave my hands up and down her, not quite knowing what her role at the hospital is.

"Is there a problem here?" The nurse says looking at this girl.

"Well, she just walked into the room and decided to tell me that I'm not good enough for my boyfriend. I'm not happy with this." The nurse glared at the girl told her to leave the room and never to step foot in the room again.

"I'm so sorry Miss-"

"Slone, Natalia Slone." Her face falls slightly, but she regains her composure. I'm happy when she recognized my name. The Slone name goes very far.

"I will make sure that she is dealt with. I'm so sorry for her mouth. She needs to keep it under control, but if you wish to make a formal complaint, I will get a form for you." I shake my head and she returns my smile and exits the room. As I'm watching the nurse leave the room I hear.

"Well, little Tally Slone grew a pair."

Oh my God Cassidy is awake.

I run out of the room shouting to the nurses that she is awake. I'm back by her side, stroking her hair and kiss her head. "Oh my God Cass, you gave us all a real good scare, dude. Don't ever do that to us again, okay? How are you feeling?" I say breathlessly. The two nurses and a rather young, but very attractive doctor comes into Cassidy's room. The hot doctor gives Cassidy an examination.

"How you feeling, Miss Blake? Are you in any pain?" He flashes his pen light over her eyes and makes her follow his finger. I reach for my phone and call her parents and Josh. The hot doctor looks at me and smiles a full, white teeth smile.

"Sorry, I haven't introduced myself. Hi, I'm Dr. Mills. Your friend is looking good. Please let me know if she needs anything." He runs his hand down my arm and a shiver escapes my body. I nod.

"I will, and thank you. Are you sure she is fine?" he smiles a sexy smile.

"I'm sure Miss. I'm sorry, I didn't catch your name"

"Oh sorry I'm Tally, Cassidy's best-friend. Nice to meet you Dr. Mills"

"Well Tally, I wouldn't say she was okay if I didn't mean it. Cassidy is fine" He smiles and turns and walks out the room, my eyes follow him out of the room, wishing that I could see what was under that white doctor's coat of his, only to be met by blue eyes gazing at me.

James is standing in the doorway wearing grey pants and a white cotton shirt, slightly tucked in with the top two buttons open. Damn, he is so freaking hot.

I smile at him and he walks towards me, but doesn't touch me, unlike every time he visited Cassidy with me.

"Hey Cassidy, glad to see you're awake. I'm James." He shakes her hand. Cassidy is speechless again. This is getting quite a habit for her. She smiles and takes his hand. James turns back to me. "Can I have a word outside please?" I look at Cassidy and she smiles and nods. I follow James out of her room and down the hall.

"You okay?" He stops and turns to me. I can't read his face. I have no clue what he is thinking.

"Not really. Do you like me Tally? I mean really like me, because seeing you flirt with the good doctor didn't sit well with me. If you're mine baby, then you're mine. I don't share with anyone." I just stand there staring into his eyes, totally shocked by his words.

What the fuck?

"I was not flirting with the good doctor, as you so politely put it, Wilde. My best friend had just woken up after being unconscious for three days. Or did you seem to forget that? He was comforting me and assuring me that Cass is fine." I take a deep breath. "Yes I like you James. I really like you, but there are things about me that you don't know, and before we could even think of going any further, you need to know them." He steps closer to me and cups my face.

"So tell me." I open my mouth to speak but close it again. James kisses my forehead. I breathe in his delicious scent, my body heating up. I love the smell of James Wilde.

"And what do you mean I'm yours? We haven't discussed anything about our relationship at all Wilde."

Chapter 7

Before he can answer my question, I hear Joe and Karen running down the hall shouting my name. "Tally, how is she?" Karen said running straight for me. I meet them at the door to Cassidy's room and smile.

"She's fine, she's smiling and talking." Karen hugs me tight and we go back into Cassidy's room.

James grips my elbow and whispers in my ear. "This conversation isn't over, you will tell me."

I give him a silent nod and I'm back by Cassidy's side. We spend the next few hours talking about what happened. Josh turned up and was all over Cass. He is still racked with guilt, no matter what we say to him. I know that Cassidy doesn't blame him. The cab driver was arrested for a DUI and a court date has been set. I yawn and Joe gives me a fatherly look.

"Okay Dad, I'm going." The sarcasm comes out just a little and we all laugh. It's nice to see my second family smiling again. James walks me to my car and I'm reminded of what James said to me upstairs.

"James, do you really want to know everything about me?" He looks at me and frowns.

"Baby, I want to know every damn thing about you, good and bad." With James saying that to me, I go up on my tiptoes and kiss his cheek. I love him calling me baby. He wraps his arms around my waist and holds me to him. "I need to kiss these again." He runs his thumb across my parted lips. I can't stop myself. I slowly lick his thumb as it passes over my lips. James groans,

I give him a shy smile, and he brings his lips to mine. We stand in the parking garage kissing. He has one arm snaked around my waist and the other hand at the nape of my neck. "So soft. I want to kiss you all over. Can I take you home Tally and stay the night with you in my arms? I want to sleep wrapped up in you." I break away from his kisses and reach for the car door. James frowns.

"See you at my place." I say before kissing him once more. His smile returns and we climb into our cars and drive off.

Everything is running through my head at hundred miles an hour. I want this, no, I need this. I can't let Dean Riley ruin my life any longer. We arrive at my place and I'm glad I can't see Scarlett's car in the drive. I had to convince her not to come to the hospital and to stay over her friend's house. Once I explained that James was with me, she backed off and knew that her baby sister was going to be okay. James was opening my car door and helping me out. He still had that look on his face like he didn't know what was going to happen. Hell, I didn't know what's going to happen.

I have to find out, right?

I turn on the lights to the kitchen. James follows me in and takes a seat at the breakfast bar. "Do you want a beer? I'm having one." I take two bottles of Budweiser out of the fridge, I hand one to James.

"Only the one, as I'm driving home." He looks at me with no expression on his face. I take a long swig of my Bud. James starts to pull the label off his bottle. I need to do something, say something. I have to get out of this black hole that Dean pushed me into.

"Then don't go home." His head shoots up and looks at me. I shrug and give him a little smile. James leaves his bottle, walks around the kitchen island, and stands right in front of me. He smells delicious.

He places his hands either side of me on the counter trapping me there. Lowering his lips to mine he kisses me softly. I put my hands on his narrow hips and pull him closer to me even more; I can feel his tight body under my hands. I can't wait to run my hands all over his body. I haven't felt like this is so long. I haven't wanted to touch another guy this way in so long.

He is kissing me tenderly, our tongues playful in each other's mouths. I can feel his erection pushing into my stomach, all I want is to free him and have him in me, and I need him inside of me. I pull away from his soft lips and hard body and take his hand and lead him up to my bedroom.

James closes the door behind us when we enter my bedroom. "Kiss me James, please.." Once again, we are face to face.

"I want to do more than just kiss you, Tally. I want to lose myself in you, baby." I open the buttons on his shirt, running my hands up his chest. I slowly push it off his broad shoulders and let it fall to the floor. I'm in awe of his body, he really works out. His upper body is perfectly toned, every muscle is defined. He has the perfect abs and that oh so delicious V shape leading down to the place I want to feel.

I noticed just below his ribs on the right side of his body James has a tattoo. 'Live & Breathe' in a very neat script. I trace my fingers over it and James smiles "For my brother, Nate." He obviously loves his brother. James also has three stars running along the top of his left shoulder.

"One star for every important person in my life. Mom, Dad and Nate. Maybe in time I can add more stars." I smile.

That is so sweet and sexy at the same time.

He kisses me again and lowers me onto my bed. He lies next to me with one leg draped between mine. I'm still wearing my shorts and t-shirt. James kisses my neck and collarbone. He runs his hand slowly down my body and stills at my hip. Panic rises in my head and my breathing is getting fast. I know I'm going to have a full panic attack.

I grip James' hand to stop him going any further. He stops kissing me, sensing that something isn't quite right. "James can we stop for a moment, I need to tell you something before we go any further." James pushes himself up on to his elbow so he is looking down on me.

"Okay. We can slow things down, I don't want to push you Tally. If it's your first time then we can wait." Oh why does he have to be so damn sweet?

"I'm not a virgin James, but thank you for offering to take things slow." I touch his face and look him in the eye "After I tell you this, I need you to understand that I.. I completely understand if you want to walk away and never look back."

I steady my breathing and begin and sit up and cross my legs. "Roughly six years ago I met this guy named Dean. He was sexy and charming and every girl wanted him, but for some reason he only wanted me. We met in college as we had a few classes together." I shrug.

"As you can gather, I'm quite a shy girl who has her defensive moments, but I was never like this, James. I was an average girl, went to parties, clubs, drank and dated boys. But Dean has changed all that."

I take a deep breath "Everything was going great for the first few months, he took me dancing and out to dinner. He made sure everyone knew that I was his. He was always branding me with hickeys, just to stake his claim. He bought me nice things, really spoiled me, even though he knew I had money."

I look down at my hands and start twisting the ring that Scarlett and Jake bought me just after the Dean incident; it was a white gold ring with a diamond heart with wings either side of it.

"Dean liked to be in control in and out of the bedroom and liked it rough from time to time, but that wasn't me and I told him often enough that I didn't like what he wanted me to do." I sigh. "We had rough sex once or twice, but this one time he really hurt me and I told him that I wouldn't do it anymore." I stop and look at James. I can't read his face, he is just staring at me with those big blue eyes. He has a pained look on his face like he knows what I'm going to say.

"That was the first night he hit me." James sucks in a huge breath, but he never takes his eyes off me. "He hit me a few times after that night but he seemed sincerely sorry after the fact. When the beatings didn't satisfy him, he turned to sex." I could see James fist's turning white as his anger grew.

"He raped you?" Tears spring to my eyes and I nod in shame. "How long did he do this to you before you told someone?"

"It happened over the next few years, but instead of being sorry he made other threats. I was too scared to leave him. It was only after a ball game that he brought two friends home with him and they had been drinking most of the day." I stop and try to control my breathing.

"Dean told me I had to have sex with his friends because they were horny and that's what good little girlfriends like me did. I told him no and that's when he tried to pin me down and hit me a few times. I managed to get away and went to Scarlett, who then contacted the police." I look up at James, who isn't looking at me. Why isn't he looking at me? Why do I feel the shame all over again? I thought this is what I needed to do to be with James.

"Why didn't you tell anyone after the first time?" I looked at him but couldn't find my voice to answer him. "Why?" This time there is anger in his voice. James had hate in his eyes, but I don't know if that hate was for me or Dean. I looked back down to my now clammy hands.

"He threatened to kill me, Scarlett and Jake. I couldn't take that risk with them; he told me he knew people that could hurt my family. James, Dean's father is a very well know in the public eye. There were rumours that he had done things in the past to get what he wants. The attacks were random, mainly after he has been drinking. Sometimes he was gentle with me, but I felt that I still couldn't stop him." James still wouldn't look at me. "James look at me, please?"

I take his hand, James's eyes soften and he looks at me. "That is why I freaked out when you kissed me the other night. The girl from Rossi's is Dean's new girlfriend, and when you were kissing me I heard her voice and Dean flashed in my head." I closed my eyes and rub my temples, I open them to look at James.

"I understand if you want to leave, just please don't contact me once you walk out the door, it will be too hard for me."

James isn't looking at me again, it's crushing my heart. My chest feels heavy and my stomach is knotting up to a painful point. I need him to look at me, but he doesn't. I climb off my bed and head to my bathroom. James stands and I think he is going to follow.

"I'm sorry Tally, for what he's done to you. Fuck! I need to get my head around this." He runs his hand through his hair.

Tears stroll down my face and I try to keep my heart from bursting through my chest. "Good bye, James. Thank you for everything." I turn and walk into my bathroom. As soon as I close the door, I breathe out a big sigh and I feel like I have been holding my breath for hours. I sink to the floor and sob, the flood gates have opened and they show no signs of stopping.

It feels like I have a ten ton elephant sitting on my chest.

There is a tap on my bathroom door. "Please just go, Wilde. I told you, I understand." I rip the towel off the rail and dry my face and praying that the water proof mascara actually works. He ignores me and pops his head around the door.

"Are you okay?" He asks and I frown.

"Do I look okay? I just told a guy who I really want to sleep with for the first time in years, that my previous boyfriend raped me. This guy can't even look at me, let alone touch me and that hurts so much. So no Wilde, I'm not okay." James comes into the room a little more, still standing and he still is naked from the waist up.

Why does he have to be so damn hot?

"How did you expect me to react Tally? It's a shock for anyone to hear that." He rubs the back of his neck. "Fuck Tally, one minute I'm thinking about how much I want to be inside of you, to taste you, and then in a full three-sixty degree turn around and you tell me that you were raped by your prick of an ex-boyfriend." He takes a deep breath "I'm sorry that my reaction has made you cry. I didn't mean to hurt you. We will get through this. I want you and I know you want me." I hold up my hands so James can pull me to my feet.

I put my hands on his hips and rub my thumbs over his skin. James holds me around my waist.

"I can't keep letting him win, James. You're the first guy I have wanted to have sex with since him. This is a huge step for me." James runs his nose along mine and breathes out a big sigh. There is his sexy smile again.

Chapter 8

I lead James back to my room and he starts to undress me. He lifts the hem of my t-shirt, lifts it over my head, and tosses it on the chair in the corner. He bends slightly and kisses my neck, just below my ear. He turns his attention to my button and zipper on my shorts, he slowly pushes them down my legs and they join my top. I'm left standing here in my purple lace bra and panties. James is on his knees before me, he places feather light kisses on my thighs.

My body is tingling all over. He trails his kisses up the thighs, skips my panties and kisses my stomach. He runs his sweet hot tongue around my navel continuing up towards my breasts. James stands, looking deep into my eyes, like he is searching for something. He kisses me then stops and speaks in such gentle tones.

"Take your bra off and lay on the bed, babe." I do has he says. I throw my bra onto the corner chair. I lay on the bed looking up at James, who is standing looking down on me. He is so hot, and I can't believe that James Wilde, new QBC superstar, is here in my room about to have sex with me.

James climbs onto my bed and lowers himself onto me; his eyes are burning into mine. He kisses my lips, my jaw, and the base of my throat. Shivers run down through me as he runs his hand down my body again, but this time he doesn't stop at my hip. His hand guides down over my panties. He looks into my eyes, trying to read me.

"I'm okay James. I wouldn't be here if I wasn't. I need this."

James trails his hand back up my body, cups my left breast, and pulls at my nipple sending a jolt through me. I can feel myself getting more and damp between my legs.

James bends his head to suck my right nipple, swirling his tongue around my nipple making it hard and longer. He pulls at my nipple with his teeth. He shifts his body down between my legs and slowly removes my now very damp panties.

"You don't need these baby, so I'm going keep them." Oh my God, did James Wilde just remove my damn panties and place them in his pants pocket? James kisses my stomach and runs his tongue from hip bone to hip bone. My body bows off the bed slightly and I let out a small moan.

"Hush baby, plenty of time for moaning. Now open for me. I need to taste you, Natalia." James parts my legs even more so he can gain access to my wet sex. My body is quivering with the thought of what Wilde is going to do to me. I can feel his warm breath on me. He is blowing on the most intimate part of my body and it feels so good. His tongue slowly flicks my clit once, twice, three times and then he glides his tongue along me with long slow strokes up and down. Still licking and sucking my clit, James slips one, then two fingers into me.

"Mmmm you taste good baby, so wet and ready for me … just for me. You know, I like this and I like you." His rhythm picks up speed, his tongue matching his fingers. My breathing hitches and he knows I'm close. "Let go, come for me baby. Let me hear you say my name, Tally." I can feel my body starting to stiffen. James sucks my clit harder and that's enough for me.

A bolt of lightning runs through my body as my orgasm takes over. "James.." My body bows off the bed, my breathing ragged. My orgasm runs on and on as James continues with his thrusting fingers. It finally stops. James covers my body with his.

"Fuck baby, you came beautifully. I so need to make that happen again. You game?" I smile, trying to get my breathing under control.

"Are you going to make me come like that every time we have sex? Well, if there is going to be other times." We both know that I have overcome my first hurdle and in my heart, I'm glad that it's happened with James. Even though I haven't known James that long, I feel strangely safe with him. It's not something I felt with Dean.

A full blown all-American smile sweeps across his face.

"Every fucking time baby. And yes there will be way more times." He winks at me. I pull him to me and kiss him, my tongue tasting my juices from my orgasm on his lips. He smiles. "You taste good, don't you?" I nod and I feel shy again. "You okay?" He asks me in a sweet gentle voice.

"I'm good James. Now are you going to make me come again or just sit there?" James eyebrows shoot up in surprise.

"Wow, who are you have what have you done to my Tally?"

My heart swells when I hear him say 'My Tally'. Am I his now? Am I his girlfriend? I reach down and between my legs to James belt and start to undo it; he suddenly shifts and stands next to my bed. I look up into his dreamy blue eyes. I shift so that I'm kneeling on my bed in front of him. I undo his button and zipper, pull his jeans and boxers down the same time, and his cock springs free.

James steps out of his jeans and boxers and kicks them to one side. He is stroking himself and it's making my body hot again. Why is it such a turn on to see him pleasure himself? I look up at James and he smiles.

"May I?" I ask him and James knows what I want.

He smiles a wicked smile and nods. I take James in my hand. He is soft, warm, and hard all at the same time. I kiss the tip of his cock and taste the small bead of dew at the tip. I kiss his whole shaft. James breathes deep.

I look up at him through my lashes and he is still smiling, so without taking my eyes off him I take him fully in my mouth and I suck slowly and softly at first, savouring him, but I pick up the pace and James starts to moan and thrust himself into my mouth.

"I have dreamt about fucking your mouth, having your soft lips wrapped around my hard cock" He tastes so good. I low growl releases from James's throat and he suddenly picks me up and pushes me back down onto the bed. "Condoms, do you have any? I need to be balls deep inside you now, baby." I point to the top drawer and James removes a small square foil packet. He sits up and opens the pack, the whole time, never taking his eyes off me for long.

Before I know it, James is back resting his body on mine. Supporting his weight on his elbow, he kisses me, his tongue invading my mouth. He stops and smiles "That mouth is such a beautiful mouth and it's all mine. No-one will get to kiss these lips but me, you understand?"

It hits me like a double decker bus. I suddenly feel panicky again, it's like Dean is talking to me. He told me I was his and no-one would ever touch me again. James kisses and I pull away slightly, James looks at me all confused.

"What's wrong? Have I hurt you?" I shift from under him and pull my knees up to my chest.

Tears slowly take over my eyes and roll down my cheeks. "I don't think this is a good idea James. I … I," I can't finish my sentence. James places his hand on my forearm and I flinch away.

"God Tally, I'm not going to hurt you, you know this. Don't let him ruin this please." He looks so pained.

I can't look at him. I can't look at his face because I know it's going to look hurt and I can't take that at this moment. I close my eyes. "I think you should leave James, it's for the best for both of us. You can have any girl you want, you're James Wilde, for fuck sake. You don't want a fucked up nobody like me." He is stunned by my words I am sure, but I can't see his face to be sure.

"I don't get what's just happened, what's changed? Did I say or do something wrong? …Tell me Tally please?" He is begging me, but I can't bear to tell him what he has done wrong. How can I tell him that a few words have put me back in shut down mode? I know that it will hurt him and I don't want that. It's easier for him to just leave; he can find a girl that's not fucked up.

"Please James, you don't want me. Go and find a girl who can give you everything." Tears stream faster down my cheeks; the lump in my throat is getting harder to fight back. James stands, pulling his boxers and jeans on.

"Don't tell me what I want. Why are you pushing me away?I have no idea what I have done, please talk to me." I can hear the anger in his voice and it scares me.

I pull the covers over me. James tries to take a step towards me but I shake my head. Without speaking, he knows not to touch me. I can't have him touching me after he said that. I can't get back into that sort of relationship. James looks deflated.

He sits at the bottom of my bed but makes to attempt to touch me. "I don't want to walk away, but by the looks on you right now, you're never going to let me love you"

I gasp "How can you say that, we have known each other for like … five minutes?" My crying has subsided slightly.

"You can't help who you fall in love with or when Tally it just happens. Don't you think we deserve a chance?" I wipe the tears from my face and sit up, holding the sheet over my body, and I know I have to tell him what he has done.

"James, what you said scared me. Dean told me all the time that I was his and he owned me. Hearing you say that was like I was right back there with him." James moved to sit next to me, looking at me like he is asking for permission.

He doesn't reach for me, just sits close. "James, I don't know if I can do this." Using his thumb and forefinger, he tilts my head to make me look at him.

He breathes out and replies, "Maybe we should take some time. I want you Tally and I'm not going to let you go that easily. I have had a taste now and I can't give that up, I won't. I will try my best to stay away while you figure out what you want to do next." His words don't sit well on my heart because I know that I might not be able to give him what he wants.

As I watch James get dressed, tear swell in my eyes again. I really don't know what I am going to do. He bends down and kisses the top of my head and whispers, "Let me love you Tally."

I look at him and he smiles even though his smile doesn't reach his eyes and then he leaves. I drag my body out of bed and get into night clothes. I make my way back to my bed, which at the moment is my solace, reach for my iPhone and put the ear phones on. I lay in my bed thinking about how I just threw away something that could have been so great. I know that it isn't James's fault, that it's mine.

I shouldn't let Dean ruin my life. I thought I could move on, but maybe I can't do that. He has moved on, but then again, he has nothing to fear. He wasn't beaten or raped by someone he thought loved him.

I still see his friends from that night, but they don't approach me. Evan and Dylan work in a sports store just a few stores away from Scarlett Avenue. Dylan just smiles at me and Evan, he can't make eye contact with me most days. When he does, I get a sympathetic smile. I feel that he is sorry about what happened but feels compelled to stick to the story they were told to say. I listen to my bedtime play list, which has soothing songs on it and I drift off to sleep thinking about how much Dean wins again.

Chapter 9

My alarm goes off and it's a bright morning. I need to get out of this bed, showered and in to work. I need to keep my mind busy so that I don't think about James. It's been four days since I saw him last and he hasn't made any contact with me what so ever. He invaded my sleep last night again, looking all hot and sexy and making love to me on a beach with the sun burning down on us. I have to shake this off. I have a fast shower and get ready for work. I can't stomach breakfast so I skip the kitchen and go straight to my car. I'm at work on time and I walk through reception, giving Bella a big hug.

"Morning, how's Cassidy doing?" I smile at her and explain that Cass is fine; she is healing and she will be back to her normal self very soon. I see Carlos and I walk over to him; he looks pissed off.

"Morning Carlos" He turns.

"Follow me, please." Great what have I done now? I know that Mrs Silver gave me a few days off due to Cassidy being in hospital, but I have worked hard since I came back, and I don't think I have done anything wrong.

I follow Carlos into his studio and he shuts the door behind me. I turn and face him, "What's this about, have I done something wrong?" A cheeky grin spreads across his face and I smile with him, my shoulders sagging in relief.

"No honey, you haven't. I just wanted to talk to you about a very big contract that we have coming up and see how Cassidy is doing?"

Ok, I'm intrigued. "Come, sit down." I follow Carlos over to the sofa in his studio and I tell him how Cassidy is doing. "Right. I know that you haven't worked for us that long, but I love your work and that isn't a secret. This contract will do Exposure and your portfolio the world of good."

I'm confused, what is Carlos actually saying? "I want you to take the new contract. Now, before you say no, let me tell you about the job first, okay?" I sink into my side of the sofa and try to take in all the information. "The contract will be with TV network QBC and we will do all the promo shots for a list of their TV shows." I lift myself up and my heartbeat quickens.

"Please don't tell me that Control is on that list." No I can't do this, I can't see James. I stand and start pacing in front of Carlos; he looks concerned.

"Tally, what's wrong? I thought you would jump at the chance to take this contract. You and James Wilde seem to have some sort of connection"

Oh God Carlos, if you only knew how much of a connection. I stop and cover my eyes. "Ok Tally, I will make this easy for you … You are taking this contract. I need you on this job. You're one of the best I have in this field, so whatever has happened, you two you need to suck it up and move on, ok?"

I have to sucked it up,

I thought to myself. I blush at the delicious memory of James on me, in my mouth, and I start to tingle. I stop and shake my head, letting out a big breath.

"Fine Carlos, I will do it, but I want a PA for this." I wince. Am I pushing my luck? Carlos looks surprised by my outburst.

"That's doable, I will give you Cleo. She's young and eager to learn" He stands and kisses the side of my head, "I'm so glad that Cassidy is doing much better." I make my way to my studio and get on with the day's work. I'm grateful I have a client full day.

Midday comes around so I stroll down stairs to Bella, who isn't at reception. That's strange for her. I check the ladies room, but no luck. I try the staff lounge but still nothing. Where is that girl? I go to Tanner's office to see if he knows where Bella is. I knock on the door gently and open it to find Tanner standing, gripping onto his desk with Bella on her knees sucking him off. I freeze. Tanner throws his head back and his eyes lock on mine. I smile and fake my shock.

"Oh my God, I'm so sorry guys. Tanner you really need to lock your door," I say with a cheeky grin on my face. Bella is as red as a tomato, and she quickly jumps to her feet but she can't look at me. Tanner slowly puts himself away and tidies up his appearance.

"We thought everyone was out to lunch, but obviously not" Tanner says calmly. Bella sits on the sofa with her head in her hands, still beaming a bright red.

"You okay, Bella?" She raises her head to look me and then to Tanner. Tanner and I burst into a fit of laughter but Bella is shaking her head at us.

Tanner says "I will go get us some lunch." I raise an eyebrow and smile a cocky smile.

"Oh, I think Bella has eaten enough for one day." She snaps her head at me and Tanner laughs and while walking towards me, we high five and he leaves his office. I sit by Bella on the sofa.

"So…you and Tanner? Nice one Bells, you're obviously are into him big time, then?" She visibly relaxes.

"Oh Tally, he rocks my world. I have liked him for a few months but never knew how he felt about me, until the night of Cassidy's accident. I know I come across all confident, but when it comes to boys I really like I have no clue. Especially with guys like Tanner fucking Black!" Oh, I know how she feels.

"Well, I know that Tanner really likes you. Carlos said that he has for a while but didn't know how to make the first move." I'm so happy that Bella can talk to me like this; I miss girl talks. As Cassidy has been healing, she gets tired real easy these days.

We chat about Tanner and boys in general; she gives me a tight hug as Tanner walks back into his office.

"Hey now ladies, I'm game for a threesome." He winks.

"Oh honey, you couldn't handle both of us, right Bella?"

Tanner laughs and sits on the floor next to the all glass coffee table and we eat our lunch, chatting and giggling. God, I have missed friends time.

It's been a nice few days at work and my weekend was busy. I had to help Scarlett run around for her birthday party, which helped with distracting me from thinking about James. I arrived to work late this morning due to an accident on my work route. I can feel my face heat up, and I know I look all flustered as I enter reception and see Bella.

"You okay? It's not like you to be late. Your QBC client's up in your studio. Just a warning … James is with them, along with a very attractive leggy piece." I blow out a big sigh and straighten myself up as I make my way into my studio. I stand outside my door and I can hear voices. I open the door and come face to face with a wall of hard, hot muscle that I know intimately. I peel my eyes up to look at him, and step back.

"Oh, umm, I'm so sorry Mr Wilde." James, who has his hands on my hips, smiles.

"Miss Slone, I was coming to see where you were." I step around James and walk to the table where there is a leggy blond and an older gentleman.

"I'm so sorry, Mr??" I don't actually know his name but I offer my hand, even though he doesn't take it.

"Mr Williams. I'm not happy that you are late to this appointment, Miss Slone. I am on a very tight schedule today." I drop my hand.

James comes back at the table and takes the chair next to Miss Leggy. I take my seat across from them and explain about the accident on my way into work. "Miss Slone, this is Carmen Vogel, she is my co-star on the show." I shake her hand and she smiles at me.

Okay, I don't know if I like her.

"So, Mr Williams, would you like to go to a location or use the studio for the stills? I'm okay with either and we have some amazing locations on file." James is staring at me with his fuck-me eyes. I bite my lip and I try not to look at him, because I know if I do, I'm going to melt. We go over the details for the photo shoot; it takes us around an hour.

"So Tally. Is it okay if I call you Tally?" Carmen asks. How did she know to call me Tally?

"Yes Miss Vogel, Tally is fine," I smile at her and she returns a full mega-watt smile back at me.

"Does a pretty little thing like you have a boyfriend?" I'm taken back by her question.

"Um, what's that got to do with the contract?" She smiles and re-crosses her long legs and places a hand on James' thigh. I clench my fists, my body heats all over, and I'm pretty sure my face gives my jealousy away.

Mr Williams stands and excuses himself. I wish Carmen would excuse herself too, so I can hash this out with James with no witnesses. Carmen leans over to James and whispers in his ear and he lets out a gentle laugh. I can feel my face burning; I need to get out of here to calm down.

"Will you two excuse me please? I will give you some privacy and I will be right back." I can't help but notice the anger in my voice. I get up to leave but James catches my elbow before I can get a grip on the door handle.

"Where are you going?" My breath hitches as I feel the warmth of his skin on mine.

"Why don't you go and sit back with Miss Vogel, you two seem quite cozy." I take a deep breath, still not looking at him. "So much for not giving up on us, Mr Wilde." He tightens his grip on my elbow.

"I meant what I said baby, I'm not giving up."

"So, what?" I wave my hands in Carmen's direction but keep my voice low so only James can hear me. "Was all that for show, you letting her put her paws on you to make me jealous, to make me see what I'm missing?" I pull my arm free and exit my studio.

I walk towards Carlos's studio with my head held high; I knock and enter when he calls out to enter. Carlos is looking over some photos on his laptop and I throw myself on the white sofa next to his desk.

"You ok Talls? You look rather flushed." I blow out a big breath and explain to him what just happened in the meeting. "You left them there?" I nod.

"Yep," popping the P as I reply. Carlos pinches the bridge of his nose and raises his head to me.

"Go back Tally, go and finish the meeting … Now." I open my mouth to speak but I see the tell-tale look on Carlos's face, so I leave and head back to my studio. I stand outside the door and take a deep breath, before opening the door and walking in. I see that James and Carmen are still seated at opposite sides of my table, deep in conversation about what I don't know, and personally don't care.

"Ah, you're back. Is everything okay, Tally?" Carmen asks with a slight smirk on her lips. I square my shoulders and reply to her.

"Everything is fine, Miss Vogel. I just needed to check with my manager about a few location possibilities." I take a seat next to James, and Carmen eyes me intently.

"Why don't you come and sit next to me Tally? I won't bite … unless you want me to," she says with a wink. I take it all in and let it wash over my head.

"I'm good here, thank you. I'm sure you would bite me if I asked, but I'm sure that Mr Wilde could bite me just as well, if not better. Don't you agree, Mr Wilde?" Carmen's face drops.

I surprised all three of us by saying that, but it felt good. Scarlett would be proud. I want James, and I know that he wants me. James looks at me with a huge grin on his face.

"Oh Miss Slone, I would be more than happy to bite you if you wish. Name the time and place and I will most definitely be there," James says matter of factly. I bite my lip and I blush right on cue. Mr Williams walks back into the room and takes a seat next to Carmen.

"So Mr Williams, are you happy to go ahead with the promo shots?" Carmen hasn't taken her eyes off me. I can feel them burning into my skull, and suddenly I feel self-conscious.

James places his hand on my left thigh with a gentle squeeze, and my breath hitches at the same time I see Carmen's eye widen. Mr Williams explains what his plans are for the promo shoot. We make our way to the door.

"Miss Slone, it was a pleasure. I look forward to working with you on this contract." We shake hands and he turns to leave. Carmen is standing there looking all goddess like, but eyes like the Hounds of Hell.

"So, James, you know Miss Slone very well then?" Oh, I'm back to Miss Slone now. James places his arm around my waist and pulls me closer.

"Yes, Carmen, I told you I was seeing someone. Tally is my girlfriend." I am taken aback by his revelation, so my body tenses and Carmen sees that.

"Maybe so James, but does she know that?" And with that she leaves the room. I pull of out James' embrace.

"Don't you think I should have a say in this? When exactly did I agree to be your girlfriend?" He blinks a few times.

"I told you, Tally, I'm not giving up on you, on us. We have something and I want it. I want it all. I don't just have sex with random women, Tally. I know that you have some underlining issues and together we will get past them." My heart tightens and I rub my chest.

I close my eyes briefly and open then to speak to James. "You really think you can get over the fact that my ex-boyfriend raped me?" I walk over to my desk without waiting for a reply. I am aware that Wilde has followed me, I can smell him and it's just the most delicious smell ever to come from a man.

He presses his body close to mine, chest to back, thighs to thighs. "It's been too long Tally, I have missed you. Have you missed me?" How could I have missed him this much, we hardly know each other? Oddly, though, I know in my heart that I have missed him just as much as he says he has missed me.

"I have missed not seeing you or hearing from you James, but you haven't answered my question." I look him in his ocean blue eyes and hold my form. I'm not backing down. He looks so lost. I can see that he is trying to find the right answer.

"James, I understand that this is hard for you, believe me I really do." I place my hand on his heart and I can feel it beating hundred miles an hour just like mine; he is warm and soft under my hand.

Oh, I want to see and feel his chest, run my hand over his stomach, to feel every defined muscle of his body. I want to smell him, take his scent in. My thoughts are halted by the knock on the door. I look up at James, who at this point looks like he wants to ravish me right here and now. Our eyes lock once more.

Chapter 10

I hear the door open, so I turn to see who is joining us in my studio. "Oh, I'm sorry, I thought you would be alone. Is everything ok in here?" Sam stands in the doorway and looks from James to me.

"It's okay Sam, Mr Wilde was just leaving." I look at James, who doesn't argue with me. He shakes Sam's hand and turns back to me.

"It was nice seeing you again; I hope to see a lot more of you. And as for our discussion ... I will, for you." He takes my hand and looks as if he's going to give me a kiss on the cheek but he places my hand over his heart and he whispers in my ear, "Does that answer your question?" James nods to both of us and leaves the studio.

I stand there staring at the door James had just left through, my heart pounding in my chest. I can't move or speak; I am momentarily paralyzed to the spot. Oh my God, he does want to try.

Sam snaps me back to the present. "You okay, Tally? You look pale. What did he say?" I blink a few times and look up at Sam trying to speak.

"He wants to try, Sammy he really wants to try." Sam leads me over to the sofa and I explain everything that has happened. From my Dean Nightmare, right up to now. Sam looks on at me in total disbelief. A tear runs down Sam's olive skinned cheek. I take his hand and cradle it in mine.

"Oh my God baby girl, how could he do that to you? And James is okay with this ... well he just declared that he is. What are you going to do, because it seems to me that you are still dealing with some issues from the dark times?" I wipe the tears away and smile at Sam.

"You have been a star Sammy, a total rock star. I haven't told a lot of people about what happened, my family and Cassidy know and that's about it. Thank you so much for understanding and for not making me feel like a victim again. I really want to be with James. I haven't wanted to be with anyone as much as I want to with him. After today I really think I could move forward with him, but I know that I still have some issues that I need to deal with." Sam hugs me and offers to take me out to dinner with him and Carlos after work.

The rest of the day goes pretty fast, as I only have a few bookings. I'm looking forward to meeting up with Carlos and Sam after work; I need to unwind after the past events.

It's Tuesday morning and I have the day off. This is why I've woken up with a slight hangover, proving that I enjoyed my evening out with the boys. I head to my bathroom and have a nice hot shower to wash away my headache and aching muscles from all the dancing we did last night. A memory runs through my head of last night and I laugh to myself. Carlos and Sammy like to dance; they wouldn't let me sit down.

I remember being in a 'Carlsam' sandwich as they liked to call it- me sandwiched between Carlos and Sam. They really helped to make me forget what had happened yesterday and the past week. I brush and dry my hair and get dressed. Scarlett is sitting on the living room floor with her birthday party plans spread out all around her. She's on the phone yet again, sorting through every detail. I join her on the floor, flicking through all the papers and forms.

While Scarlett is on the phone, it gives me a chance to call Cassidy. I gather my phone out of my bag. Cassidy answers on the third ring, "Hey, Talls! You okay, babe?" My hearts swells at the sound of my best friend's voice; she sounds happy which makes me happy.

"Hey Cass, I'm good. How are you feeling? Still getting the headaches?" She has been suffering with them since the accident; the Doctor said it was common.

"I'm getting there, one day at a time Talls. I'm not getting them as much as I was, which a good thing I guess is. How's work? More importantly, how's Mr Wilde?" I thought about what to tell her, should I lie not to upset her or should I tell her the whole truth? I haven't spoken to James since he left the studio yesterday afternoon.

I was glad in a way, as I didn't know what to say to him. "Work is going great. I went out with Carlos and Sam last night; had a tad too much to drink." I went silent, but Cassidy didn't leave the gap in chat for too long.

"And? … Don't leave me hanging Talls, give it up. What happened? I need a night out." I look at Scarlett, who is deep in her conversation on the phone.

"Hang on Cass, let me go outside." I walk out to the front porch of our house and sit on the top step. It's a good thing we live in a very high security gated community, thanks to my dad.

"Okay, don't freak because I haven't told you before today, okay?! Promise me, Cassidy."

"I promise now … Spill Missy." I take a deep breath and close my eyes.

"I almost had sex with James last week…" Cassidy cuts me off.

I pull the phone from my ear. "YOU WHAT? And why exactly am I only now hearing about this?" I cut her off this time.

"You promised, Cass!" I can hear her sigh on the other end of the phone.

"I'm sorry Talls, carry on."

I sigh, "Everything was going good but I stopped him and told him everything about Dean. I told him I understand if he walks away."

"Did he, I mean, did he walk away?" She asks.

"Not at first, we talked a little more and we tried again. Oh Cass, I really want him. He makes me feel safe and sexy at the same time." I look down at the step just beneath me.

"So why not at first, Tally what did he do to you?" I could hear the anguish in her voice.

"Nothing Cass, it was all me, okay? Well, sort of. He was kissing me after a few things had happened…." Cassidy cut me off again.

"What few things? Come on Talls, don't hold back. I need all the hot gossip, you know we can talk about all these things." I blush again, even though I know that Cassidy can't see me.

"Fine, you sex freak. He went down on me okay. And … I gave him a blowjob. Are you happy now?" I smile.

"Yes, actually. So, is he big?" I can hear her laughing.

Shocked by her reply, I exclaim, "Cassidy Blake, you have such a dirty mind! Get your mind out of the gutter!" I swear I can hear her smiling. "I'm not giving you that much detail, Cass. Anyway, where was I? Yep, he started kissing me again and started talking to me, saying things."

I pause and close my eyes, "Things Dean used to say to me and I freaked out again. He tried to calm me but it was best we cut contact for a while and he left." I open my eyes to find James standing in front of me and I freeze. I can hear Cassidy on the other end calling my name; I finally find my voice.

"I'll call you later, okay? I have to go. I love you." With that, I hang up.

I look up at James standing there in black jeans, white t-shirt and black blazer, looking sexy as fuck. He is smirking at me and it gets me thinking, was he standing there when I said that last bit to Cassidy? "Hi."

"Hi yourself," James says back to me. Why is he here? "You look rough, you okay?"

"I'm fine Wilde, just a little hung-over. I went out with Carlos and Sam last night, drank too much, again. Why are you here?"

I look down at my hands and twist my sibling ring again. James steps closer and places his hand over mine; he is kneeling on the step before me.

"Let me in baby, please" I can tell by his eyes that he truly wants in.

"Get off the ground, James." I pat the step next to me for him to sit. He sits as close as he can to me and puts his arm around my waist, pulling me even closer.

"I had a long talk with Sam yesterday and told him everything ... about Dean... me and you." I turned away from him and looked across the street to watch the children in my street having a water fight. They are laughing and screaming, water balloons flying everywhere. The boys are chasing the girls with water pistols.

"Sam told me that he thinks I need to give us a chance, see how things work out... I think he might be right." I turn back to James, who is now wearing his All-American-Smile and I blush but smile back at him. "I can't keep letting him win, I need to take the next step and I want that step with you James. I know I have told you this but now I'm going to show you."

We are still face to face but neither of us moving, just smiling at each other. I have to taste those lips again so I make the first move. I learn forward and cup his face, rubbing his cheek with my thumb and kiss his soft lips. Soft, slow kisses follow; James places his hand on my left thigh, rubbing slowly. We kiss for how long I don't know. Time passes but all that matters is James and me.

I hear giggling and we break our kiss, only to find three young boys aiming their water pistols at us both. I turn to find James smiling a wicked smile at the boys. Oh no, I know where this is going.

I turn back to the boys, knowing one of their names, only because I babysat a few times for his family.

"You wouldn't dare Seth, don't even think about it, kiddo." All three boys open fire on me and James. I jump up, squealing like a girl and James runs towards the boys, who turn and run across the street.

I turn and run into my kitchen and rummage through the cupboards to look for our water pistols that Josh and Lucas had left from the last time the street had a water fight. I find the three water pistols and fill them; I turn to leave the kitchen with full water pistols in hand to find Scarlett changed and ready to get wet.

I hand one to Scarlett. As we walk through the living room, we can hear the joyful screams from the street children. We enter the street and water is flying everywhere, even parents are now involved. Children are chasing adults and the adults are chasing children; everyone having fun in the sun. Both Scarlett and I walk towards the sidewalk with water pistols on hand and full to the top.

All the girls and their moms run in our direction and stand by our sides. All the boys line up across the street, including James Wilde.
He has removed his blazer and his white tee is slightly wet, clinging to his beautiful chest and stomach. I chuckle. So that's the plan, boys V girls.

James has acquired a pistol from one of the boys, who look quite confident that they are going to win this water fight. We shall see.
One of the dads shouts, "Get em!" At the same time, all the boys and men run forward towards us ladies.

We stand our ground and wait until they get closer. As the boys are running, they are firing their water pistols and us ladies know that they will run out of water pretty soon after they reach us. I wait with the girls until the boys are about eight feet in front of us, then Scarlett yells.

"Go Go Go!"

We all surge forward spraying water at the boys and everyone is getting soaked. I go straight for little Seth, who is trying to catch his mother.

I get him and he falls to the floor, pretending to be a wounded soldier. I get hit right on my ass, and spin to find Wilde standing there blowing invisible smoke from his water pistol.

"Gotcha baby … right on that sexy little ass of yours." I can see lust and desire in his eyes as he scans my body to find that my camisole is almost see through, due to all the water coverage from this water fight. I'm wearing my denim shorts and a white camisole with a Peace sign printed on the front and now my baby blue bra is almost visible. I walk over to James who hasn't taken his eyes off me.

I go up on my tip toes and kiss him; he kisses me back and that when I make my move. I step back and let him have it. I empty my water pistol on his body. He looks so good wet, his hair is damp in some places but his t-shirt is now very wet and see through and clinging to his perfect upper body even more. He stumbles back laughing, and he lunges for me. Just touching my arm, I manage to escape and dart for my house. Leaving everyone out in the street, James follows me into the kitchen.

I put the kitchen island between us. I smile at him and he returns a cheeky grin. "Do you honestly think that I won't catch you, baby?" He moves around the island to get closer to me, but I step to the side also.

"We shall see Mr Wilde, what do you intend to do with me once you catch me?" Old Tally is seeping through and I don't intend to stop her. I see my favorite smile spread across his face. He darts for me again, but I move out of his reach and run up the stairs.

Chapter 11

I make it to my bedroom and try to close the door but James gets to my room just as I'm closing it. He catches the door, walks into my room and closes it behind him. I start walking backwards but James catches me by my waist. I place my hand on his forearms and reach up to kiss him, soft at first but James deepens our kiss. My hands travel up to his head; I love running my fingers through his hair.

His hand slides up to cup my ass and he pulls me closer to him. I can feel his erection pushing into my stomach, and I lift the hem of his wet clingy t-shirt. I can't full lift it over his head, as I'm a short-ass, so he does it for me. He drops it on the floor and kisses me again, our tongues playing with each other, tasting. I moan and James peels my soaking wet top up over my breasts, shoulders and my head and it joins his t-shirt on the floor.

His hands rest on my hips, his thumbs stroking my bare skin. I feel for his button and zipper without breaking our kiss. I slip my hand down his jeans and boxers at the same time and find he is hot and hard and ready for me.

I grip his cock and run my hand up and down him. A small moan breaks from James's throat and I inhale his pleasure, which sends my body racing even more. I push his jeans and boxers down to the floor and James steps out of them. I give him a sweet smile and kneel before him, looking up at him through my lashes with his cock in one hand.

"Oh, how I have missed your mouth baby, I have been waiting for you to lick me with that delicious tongue of yours." I lick the whole length of his shaft; I had forgotten how big he is. Oh, he tastes so good.

I flick my tongue over the head where a bead of pre-cum has formed. I take him slowly into my mouth, until I have him all inside me and I can feel him at the back of my throat. I suck slowly at first, but then begin to pick up speed.

He thrusts his hips so that he is fucking my mouth, "Oh God baby … so good. I don't want to come in your mouth Tally … Stop baby!" I pull back and stand to face him again. He kisses me, his tongue invading my mouth.

He starts to trail kisses down my neck, down to my breasts, his hands expertly un-clipping my bra, where it joins our clothes on the floor. James is completely naked but I'm still wearing my shorts and panties. James drags his teeth along my earlobe and trails kisses down my collar bone to the base of my neck. A shiver runs through my body.

"If you keep shivering at my every touch, I'm not going to last Tally." He cups my breast and pulls at my nipple. I arch my back while he takes my other nipple in his hot wet mouth. His tongue, running circles around my nipple, is making my body hotter, He continues down my stomach, kissing, licking and sucking as he goes. I place my hands on his shoulders, his skin hot under my fingers. He reaches my hip bone and nips it with his teeth and I cry out with both pleasure and pain. James looks up at me through his lashes and smiles his sexy smile,

"You like that?" I look down at him and nod with a smile spread across my face.

He unbuttons my shorts and leisurely pulls my zipper down. He hooks both thumbs into my shorts and panties and slides them down my thighs, to my ankles, "Step out baby."

I do as he says, still holding his shoulders to balance myself. I have come this far and I'm feeling an overwhelming surge of pride in myself.
I can do this, I won't let that scumbag win anymore. James kisses the inside of my thighs, left first, then right and I can feel my knees getting ready to buckle.

"James …" He stops kissing me and his blue eyes look at me.

"Are you okay? Do you want me to stop? It's okay if you do baby, I don't want to push." I smile and I can know that I'm falling for him. Hard. My head and my hearts know this. I place my hands either side of James's face.

"James I'm fine, I'm more than fine. Can we move to my bed? I don't think my legs will support me when I come" He smiles and my James is back. He stands and lifts me and within a few seconds I'm lying on my bed with James resting between my legs.

"Open up for me baby, I need to taste my favorite flavor"

He kisses my thighs slowly and seductively until he reaches my sex. His hot tongue finds my clit, and he slowly runs his tongue up and down, round and round making my body bow off the bed; I fist my hands in his hair and hold him tight to me. I can hear him moan slightly and I know that he is enjoying me.

"You smell like pineapple baby. Fucking delicious." I am all sensation. The joyful sounds from the street have faded from my hearing. It's just James and me in our own little world. My room could be anywhere in the world and I wouldn't know it as long as James Wilde was making love to me.

I feel two fingers slide into me and the sensation doubles. I can feel my body starting to tremble. James picks up the speed of his fingers sliding into me and I know that I will come pretty soon. With James' fingers and tongue assault my clit, my body trembles even more and when James just grazes my clit with his teeth it's enough to send my body into a delicious spiral of sensation.

"Oh God...James...So good" My body bows off the bed again, I have a fist full of sheet, all the while James continues finger fucking me and slows the pressure on my clit until I can't take anymore.

"STOP!"

I scream. I'm panting, trying to slow my breathing. James slides up my body. Wow, that was amazing; by Christ does he know what he is doing! "I couldn't take anymore, that was intense … Wild even." I smile at him and bite my lip.

"Apt description," James smiles and covers my body with his and kisses me deeply again. "So, you liked that?" I smile and nod. "Are you okay, baby? Do you think you're ready for us to take the next step?"

I know I'm ready, this is a huge leap for me but I need to take it. My life can't be put on hold any longer. James's touches will erase Dean's.

"James, I want to take this step with you, fuck me please." He shakes his head with a little chuckle.

"No baby, I don't want to fuck you. I want to make love to you for the first time, but believe me baby, it most certainly won't be the last." He kisses me and our tongues dance in each of our mouths.

I hand him a condom from my bedside table. James rolls the condom on and places himself between my legs. He holds his weight on his elbow, looking down on me.

"If you want to stop at any time just tell me, okay?" I nod, my breathing slightly ragged and I'm unsure whether it's from fear or lust. James slowly sinks into me and I close my eyes, taking him one inch at a time. He sinks fully into me but he stops. I still have my eyes closed and I feel James' soft lips on mine.

"Tally, look at me baby." I open my eyes to look at the biggest bluest eyes I have ever seen and they are looking deep into my soul. "You okay? I'm going to move."

I smile. "I'm okay, take me slowly at first." He bends to kiss me and with his lips soothing mine, He starts to move, our eyes locked. We are fully connected and I realize that James Wilde wants me, all of me. The good and the bad.

This is where I want to be.

James moves slowly in and out of my wetness, and it feels so good to be here with him right at this moment. "Fuck baby you feel so good, so tight. Perfect fit for me. Say my name, Tally." I give him a sweet smile, and I know that I'm safe with him. James won't hurt me, he loves me. Fuck. James Wilde loves me.

I touch James' face and he smiles at me, while sticking to his slow leisurely pace. It feels amazing to have him fill me, to have him make me want him more than any man ever has before.

"Faster James … faster please," I beg, the slow pace is killing me. He doesn't have to be told twice. James picks up the pace of his thrusts.
He is making love to me like it's our last night together. James groans and shifts his body so he can apply pressure on my clit.

"I want us to come together baby." My breathing is staggered at the same time as that delicious sensation builds inside me yet again. James picks up speed and I let go.

"I'm coming James! Oh God. James. Fuuuuck" My body tenses around his cock inside me and it set his orgasm off. It feels like our orgasms go on forever until James stills, eyes locked, ragged breathing and falls to my side.

"Wow baby, that was epic. I have never come so hard in my life." He turns to face me like he has just found out something special. "It's you, you do this to me." I smile at him and we both lay there trying to steady our breathing. James is lying next to me with his head on my shoulder and his arm draped over my stomach.

He is running his fingers around my navel which tickles and I giggle. I run my fingers through his damp hair and he kisses my neck. This is nice. James has made me forget why I was so scared in the first place. He has lifted my spirits and I feel lighter in myself.

I fight to hold the tears back but I start to cry and I try to wipe the tears away before James sees. I fail miserably and James twists his body to look at me. We are now eye to eye,

"Oh no baby don't cry. Please. What's wrong?" I stroke his cheek and trail my thumb across his bottom lip; these lips are mine.

"James I never thought I would get to this point in my life again, but you helped me here and I will always be grateful to you for that. I enjoyed every second of it and yes I would do it again but only with you. This means so much so much, it's indescribable" He gives me a sexy grin.

"Well I'm glad that it was with me and yes I will be the only guy to make love to you from today onwards. You are mine Natalia Slone and I'm yours … always" I kiss him and the tingling feeling sweeps through my body again but I hold it back just for now.

James has helped me overcome the biggest fear of my life and I owe him to try. It still lingers with me as to why James Wilde, Hollywood's newest TV superstar, wants me but that is for another day to question.

We fall asleep holding each other like we have done it a thousand times before; it feels effortless and natural to be here with him. Not sure how long we sleep for but I wake to find that we have moved while sleeping. I am now facing James' back with my arm draped over his waist, and James has his arms draped backwards over my hip. I kiss the space between his shoulder blades, his skin hot and slightly salty from sweating after our amazing love making. I place his arm over his body and slowly climb out of bed.

I need to pee. I stand in my bathroom looking at my reflection in the mirror. I would say I looked the same but I don't. My cheeks are flushed and my hair looks like I have been dragged through the bushes, but I'm holding my head high. I'm not moping anymore; there's happiness in my face that hasn't been there is such a long time. It's all thanks to one Mr James Wilde. I'm wearing James's white t-shirt, which is now dry from the earlier street water fight and a pair of my boy shorts.

I walk back into my room and watch James sleep in my bed. God he looks like an Angel when he sleeps. My Angel. I stand there just looking at him when I see my phone lights up, letting me know I have a text. I quietly walk towards my bedside table and pick up my phone. The text is from Cassidy.

Cassidy: You didn't call me back, bitch!!!

Me: Sorry, Wilde popped around ;)

Cassidy: Did you fuck him?? TELL ME NOW!

Me: Yes, details later. He is lying in my bed sleeping. Love you

Cassidy: Whore. But I love you. Send me a pic NOW!!!!

I giggle quietly and snap a picture of James sleeping. He is lying on his stomach now but he is facing me. The sparkle from the fair lights are giving a small amount of glow on his body and face. Just enough to show off his beautiful body, the sheet sitting nicely on the bottom of his back. I hit send and it takes Cass seconds to reply.

Cassidy: You lucky bitch, WOW! Tally you have yourself a freaking sex god. Whoop, Go Tally ;)

Me: Hahaha night doll. I'm going back to bed. Love you. X

Cassidy: Night. Love you

She is such a nut but I love her with all my heart.

Chapter 12

I make my way down to the kitchen. It's dark outside now and Scarlett is sitting at the dining table on her laptop. I blush even without her looking at me. "Hey Scar, what are you up to?" I startle my sister with my sudden question.

"Oh God, Pup, you scared the shit out of me!" She looks me up and down, smirks at me and I know that she knows what's happened. "I've had an email from the artist I want to perform at my party." I clap my hands together like a five year old having a lollipop.

"What did they say, are they going to show up?" She smiles and I already know the answer.

"Yep! The fee has been agreed to, so I'm one happy Scarlett. Just like you are one happy Pup." I hug her and try to read her email but she closes her laptop. I sit down and wait for the sisterly questions. Shit. "So Pup, you okay?" I frown.

"Yeah! Why would you think I'm not?" She looks me up and down, waving her hand at my clothes, or lack thereof. "Oh! Umm yeah, James is upstairs sleeping in my bed." I look shyly down at the hem of James' t-shirt. Scarlett lifts my chin up so that I'm looking at her.

"Tell me, Pup" I shrug.

"We had sex. Well, he made love to me." Scarlett takes hold of my hands in hers and goes into Big Sister mode.

"Are you okay? How did it go? Okay, you don't need to go into full detail, but I want to know Talls." I blush again and smile at the memories.

"It was good Scar, he took care of me. He went slowly; he kept asking me if I was okay. He was so gentle until I asked him to speed things up," I smile but look at the pattern on the birthday file in front of me.

Looking anywhere but my sister's face, as I'm nervous at her upcoming reaction. "Natalia Slone, you little minx. Good for you, Pup. It's about time. We thought you would never move past this. And to think it was with James Wilde." She hugs me and I can hear James coming down the stairs.

I flash a whole new shade of red. He enters the kitchen wearing just his jeans, bare feet and bare upper body, since I'm wearing his tee. God, he is sex on legs.

"Evening ladies." He walks further into the kitchen and kisses me on the head, "Evening baby, my tee looks good on you."

"Evening James, you sleep okay? I didn't want to wake you." I turn back to Scarlett, who hasn't taken her eyes off James's body. I nudge her and she blinks and looks at me with a huge grin on her face.

She mouths "WOW" at me.

"Are you ladies hungry? I could pop out for some food or I could cook us something." I look at Scarlett and we both burst out laughing. James looks at us, confused.

"Sorry James, Tally and I find it strange that a guy wants to cook for us, but you can if you want to. It gives me time to show my baby sister what she will be wearing to my birthday party." She gives me a sly smile as she knows I'm dreading this. I don't do heels.

I roll my eyes at Scarlett, "Great! Here we go again," I shake my head at my sister.

"When is the party, Scarlett?" James asks. Scarlett looks at me and I shrug.

"It's in December. I'm having a cocktail theme. Evening gowns and tuxes." James nods.

"Sounds like fun. Oh speaking of parties, Tally I'm going to the wrap party for Season One; I want you to come with me. It's nothing fancy, just the cast and crew having a party with lots of drinks and a big buffet." I look at Scarlett, who is nodding, telling me to say yes.

"When is it?" James comes to sit at the table with a glass of orange juice.

"A week this Friday, are you free?" I can feel Scarlett's hand on my thigh, giving me a-you-will-be-fine look.

"Yeah. I'll come with you."

"I thought you just did?" He smirks and winks at me and Scarlett bursts out laughing while I turn blood red and cover my face with my hands. I smack his chest, as he gets up to cook for us all.

I can't believe he just said that in front of my big sister. He is lucky that he didn't say that in front of Jake. Oh God Jake; what will my brother think of James and my parents. I haven't dated since Dean. I know that my parents will go easy on him but Jake will go all big brother and protective. I understand why he will be like that after what I've been through in the past. James is cooking us all something to eat while I sit with Scarlett at the table as she opens a page on her Mac and shows me a stunning dress for her party.

I'm pleasantly surprised that I like it and then she shows me the shoes. "Scarlett, I won't be able to walk in those! Please, can we go for a smaller heel? I will do anything else, just please pick a smaller heel."

I look at my sister, pleading with her and I pout. "Oh Pup don't look at me like that. No pouting, you know how it effect's me." Yes! It worked; I mentally high five myself.

"Fine Pup, I will look for a smaller heel, okay?" I wrap my arms around her shoulder and give her a squeeze.

"Thank You Scar," I bounce over to James who is finishing up our meal. "What are you cooking?" I ask, while I sit on the counter.

"Chicken wraps with peppers, onion and mushrooms. I assumed since they were in the fridge that you both liked them. Oh shit, do you both like all this stuff?" I smile.

"Yeah babe, it's fine." James's head snaps up at me in surprise that I just called him 'babe.'

I smile at him and he returns a sexy smile. This feels nice. It feels strange to feel this happy again but I don't want it to change; it feels good. James turns and stands between my legs, puts his hands on my ass, and slides me closer to him. He kisses me slowly, licking my bottom lip. I can feel his smile while he is kissing me. I pull away

"So what do I have to wear to this wrap party?"

James shrugs "Whatever you want." Scarlett darts over to us.

"James, don't tell her that. She will go in jeans and Converse. We will look for something at the store tomorrow, okay?"

I nod. I like some of the clothes we sell at Scarlett Avenue and I know I won't have to pay for any of it. Perks of the being the owner's little sister. The three of us eat the chicken wraps that James made for us and they are delicious. We chat about the wrap party and Scarlett's party.

"Jeans and Chucks are fine with me as long as I get to show you off to all my friends. You can meet my best friend Marcus, he is a legend. All the ladies love him. He is hot, single and likes to party." I look at Scarlett, who has risen from her birthday folder, to take in all this info on Marcus.

"What does he look like, you know since you said he is hot?" I smile at him.

"Why? Have you had enough of me already, baby? Did you not enjoy yourself upstairs?" I whip my head back to face him.

"JAMES!!!" He smiles his sexy smile at me. "Really, my big sister is sitting right there. Do you have to tell her about our sex life?" Scarlett just smiles at the both of us.

"She has a point James, what does Marcus look like? How old is he? Come to think of it how old are you Mr Wilde?"

He takes a sip of his water and answers our questions, "Both Marcus and myself are twenty-five. He is my BFF, as you girls would say." He laughs and shakes his head, "We have been friends since we were three years old; his parents moved into the house next door to ours. We hit it off and have been friends ever since. Scarlett, for your main question. Marcus is six feet tall, give or take an inch, with dark hair a bit longer than mine, and green eyes. Is that to your liking?" Scarlett's face is a picture; I could have sworn she was drooling.

I reached over the table and closed her mouth, which in turn she snatched her head away.

"Any tattoos? Oh, I love a man with tattoos," Scarlett swoons.

James smiles. "Yeah, he has tattoos. So am I going have to fight you off, since I have two tattoos?"

Scarlett looks at me and then back to James "I see. Can I have a closer look?" Oh great, here we go. Scarlett has a big weakness for men with tattoos. Every boyfriend she has had; has had a tattoo. James stands and Scarlett comes around the table to meet him.

Scarlett moves in closer, and she goes to run her hand over my boyfriend's ribs. "Scarlett, don't you dare, that body belongs to me." I shake my head at her and she quickly puts her hand down. I look up at James and he is smiling at me, so I wink at him. Scarlett is still hovering, "Live & Breathe."

She looks up at James, "I don't get it, what's it mean?"

Before James can answer "It's for his brother Nate." James smiles, leans over and kisses the top of my head before sitting back down next to me. Scarlett looks confused. I'm not confused, but I don't know the reason behind the tattoo. I hear James take a deep breath.

"Scarlett, the tattoo is for my little brother Nate. Nate died when he was six years old from cancer." Both Scarlett and I gasp.

Scarlett looks at me, "Did you know about this?" I shake my head, too afraid to speak; I can feel the burn in my eyes. Scarlett stands and packs her planner away.

"I think you to need to talk before you tell me anything, I'm going to bed. James if you're staying, I will see you in the morning," and with that she leaves us alone in the kitchen. I take James' hand and lead him into the lounge.

We sit on the large L shaped sofa facing each other. "Tell me about Nate." He smiles and takes my hand.

"I was eleven at the time but we were very close. We did almost everything together, that we could do anyway. He was ill for a while and the chemo worked for a small time but Nate got sick again and went downhill pretty fast. I still remember coming home from school that day. My dad was sitting on the front porch and I could tell he had been crying." He shook his head like he was trying to get rid of the picture in his head.

"James, if it's too hard we can stop." I grab a hold of his hand.

"God, what did I do to deserve you? You need to know Tally, if we are going to make a go of this. I want you to know."

I smile and kiss the back of his hand. "I came home from school one day and had a stomach ache most of the day, but didn't really think anything of it. I just went through the motions of my school day. When I got off the school bus I had a feeling of dread hit me but didn't fully know why. When I saw my father, I knew in my heart that Nate was gone. I remember screaming, dropping my school bag and running for my house. My father held me tight but I needed to see my brother." He took in a big breath, "After some time, we walked into the house. I remember how quiet the house was, how it smelled."

A shiver runs through his body and I take that as my cue to climb into his lap. He wraps his arms around me, holding me tight to him. I kiss his neck and a small groan escapes from his mouth. I kiss him again and trail my kisses up to his ear, grazing my teeth across his earlobe; he tenses and tightens his grip on me. I smile against his hot skin.

James moves so that I'm now lying beneath his perfect body on the sofa. He runs his fingers down my cheek and I can't help but lean into his hand. My heartbeat quickens and it's from his touch. His lips brush mine, and I part my lips, inviting his tongue to play with mine.

Our kisses deepen and my body heats with sexual awareness for James. I feel my way up from his wrist to his elbow, up to his shoulder until I find his hair. His soft hair. James' hand trails down my body from my face, across my shoulder, and down my arm. He stops at my wrist and pulls away from my lips to plant a sweet gentle kiss on the inside of my wrist. He smiles at me with his devious smile.

"Do you know how beautiful you are Tally? How amazing you smell?" All I can think to say is, 'Oh, you smell good too Wilde.' A shy smile slips across my face as I pull him back to my lips. I can taste him and smell him and it's a head rush. How can James do this to me, to my body? He can make me forget everything in the world. I can now, for the first time since Dean, can see my future with someone.

I could see myself making a life with James but can James see that with me? My heart skips a beat. I place my hand on James's and run it along the side of my body, down past my hip and around to my ass.

Chapter 13

Wednesday morning was the best morning for as long as I could remember. Waking up next to James Wilde, in my bed after a very hot but sensual night of love making, was amazing. We made love twice. Each time James was gentle with me, planting soft kisses all over my body, cherishing every inch of me. We even talked more about my situation with Dean and how things went down in my life after that dark time. From the delicious memories I can feel my blush creep over my face and chest. I'm sitting in the staff lounge at Exposure, sipping at my tea when Carlos and Sam walk in. They take one look at me and smiles appear on both their faces.

"So Miss Tally, what did you do on your day off? Or should I say who did you do?" I gasp and look at Sam, who has the most ridiculous smile on his face. Carlos sits in the chair next to me.

"So by the look on your face, you sorted things with James." I nod, still blushing.

"See, I told you," Sam says over his shoulder, while making coffees for himself and his lover.

I roll my eyes, "Yes Sammy, you did."

Carlos looks at me with caring eyes "Are you both okay? Did you talk or just fuck? I don't know what's gone on between you two but there is something there." I'm not sure how much Carlos knows about my past, but I can only assume that Sam has told him some details. I place my mug on the table and tuck my hair behind my ear, sitting back in my seat and looking at Carlos.

"We talked … a lot Carlos. It was good. We both got a lot off our chests. He told me about his brother who died when he was younger. It was nice."

I can see Sam giving me that you're-not-telling-us-everything look. My heart rate picks up and a smile at the boys. "God! Sammy, do you have to look at me like that?" I blush yet again.

"Yes Talls; c'mon girl, don't leave anything out." I sigh and Carlos looks at his boyfriend, giving him a look.

"Yes Sam, we fucked okay. Is that what you want to hear?" We all burst out laughing. From behind us, I hear a familiar voice.

"Well, I thought we made love, but fucking is good too, as long as it's with you." I spin around to find James leaning against the door frame and I blush a whole new shade of red. Where the hell did he come from? I can't pull my gaze from his and he walks further into the room and sits next to me, not taking his eyes off mine.

He leans in and gives a full James Wilde kiss, full of passion. Wow. We pull apart and I look at Carlos and Sam and I can't believe what I'm seeing; both Carlos and Sam are blushing. So it's not just me that James effects, Thank god. I look at James and I'm wondering why is he here.

"What are you doing here?" James smile and fakes a hurt expression.

"Can't a guy come and visit his girlfriend at her work place?" My heart skips a beat from the word 'girlfriend.' I look at James confused, and he frowns back at me; my happy loving mood just took a nose dive.

"That's our cue babe, let's leave these two to it." I watch as Carlos and Sam leave me alone in the lounge with James. Why does it shock me when he says the word 'girlfriend?'

"Why are you still having trouble with me calling you my girlfriend, Tally? I thought after last night we would have been able to get past this." I play with my ring again, it's a nervous habit and I can tell that James is catching on about it. "Why are you nervous baby? Talk to me please."

Taking a deep breath I look up at James, his eyes searching mine. His hair is still perfectly styled but he is looking all boyish, even though he is twenty-five. He is wearing faded blue jeans and a tight blue v-neck t-shirt. He is just simply hot.

"It scares me, being someone's girlfriend again. I know that you won't hurt me James, believe me I know." I touch his thigh and I can feel the heat radiating through his clothing. "Give me time and I will get used to it." I give him a pleading look and he smiles at me. "James, I'm trying, okay?" I kiss him and I know instantly that it was a mistake.

James deepens his kiss and pulls me onto his lap so that I am straddling him, one hand on my ass and the other trailing up my back under my shirt. Both of my hands are around his neck holding him to me, tugging at his hair slightly and James moans into my mouth, which sends hot burning shivers down my spine.

It suddenly hits me that I'm at work, not good. I pull my face away but stay seated on his lap, feeling his arousal between my legs. I sigh heavily, as I don't want to stop, "James we need to stop, I'm at work." James trails soft kisses down my neck, making me burn for him even more. I go to climb off but he stills me.

"Just a few more kisses please? You know you want to." His sexy smile makes my mouth go dry, as I want to kiss him more, but I know that we should stop.

"I do want to James, but you have to go; my client will be here shortly. I will text you later, okay?" I reluctantly climb off him and pull him to his feet. He towers over me and bends down to kiss me goodbye. I walk James down to reception and I can see Bella staring at us. She smiles at me and I can't help but smile back at her. James has his arm around my waist, holding me to him. As we hit reception, Mrs Silver enters through the main door and I pull out of James' grip. I try not to look at him, but I know he is staring at me.

"Good afternoon, Mrs Silver. How are you today?" She smiles at me and shakes her head.

"How many times Tally? Please call me Erica." She glances at James and frowns. "Mr Wilde, did we have a meeting today?" I look at James who still has his eyes on me. I see hurt in them. Fuck.

Without looking at Erica, James replies, "I just came to visit Tally … Sorry Miss Slone." Oh Miss Slone, fuck he called me Miss Slone. I just know that he is pissed off by me pulling away. I didn't know how Mrs Silver would have reacted; I don't know what the policy is about staff dating the clients. Carlos hasn't said anything. In fact, he pushed for me to be with James.

"I think we're done, so I was just leaving." Without saying goodbye, or even looking at me, James leaves and my heart sinks. Mrs Silver leaves to go to her office and my legs feel like they are going to buckle beneath me. I feel arms wrap around my waist and hold me, leading me to one of the back rooms. They sit me on the sofa and kneel in front of me. Only then do I see that it's Tanner.

"Get her a glass of water, Bella. Tally, can you hear me? Talls, blink sweetie, please." I blink a few times and Tanner visibly relaxes. Bella hands me a glass of water and the ice bobs in the glass.

"Tally, are you okay?" I shake my head. I have just upset my, well, I'm not actually sure what James is to me now. Have I just thrown away the one thing that was good for me? My chest tightens to think that James might have walked away from me for good.

A chill runs down my spine and Tanner rubs my arms. "I think James just walked out on me. I...I didn't know how Erica would feel about us being together. About James being my ... boyfriend" Oh God, did I just say that? I did. I have just admitted that James Wilde is MY boyfriend.

Tanner smiles at me and looks at Bella then back to me, "Feels good, doesn't it? Finally, admitting that Wilde is yours." I nod and my smile grows bigger.

"Thank you, you two. For being my friends. Speaking of you two, how are you doing?" Bella blushes and Tanner strokes her bare leg as she sits next to me.

"We're good" He nods proudly at Bella, who flashes him a seductive smile.

"I'm so happy for you guys." I genuinely was happy for them, and I plastered on a smile, even though my heart was breaking quietly. After my afternoon clients I was finished for the day, so I decide to stop by Scarlett Avenue to visit my sister. I step into the shop with my forced smile again. The shop is quiet, just a few customers. Scarlett is finishing up with a customer, when she sees me and smiles her big sis smile.

I walk over to the counter and give her a hug. "How are you doing, pup? Work okay?" I nod.

"Work is great, been busy all day today. It's all good." I smile. "You been busy today?" I gesture at the store.

"It's been the usual, to be honest. I have done a lot for my party, though. The girls have handled the store today. You okay Pup, you don't seem right?"

I shrug "I'm good Scar."

"So let's go and have a look at what you're going to wear for the wrap party." Oh God, I had forgotten that. It's been a few hours since I have heard from James. Do I text him, ask him if we are okay, asking if I'm still invited to the wrap party?

My stomach knots just thinking that he doesn't want me to go with him and I imagine him going with someone else. No! James wouldn't do that, he promised not to give up on me. On us. But the way he was looking at me in work this afternoon, I really don't know what he is feeling or thinking right now.

Maybe I should text. "I'm going send a quick text first then we will have a look at some clothes, okay?" I leave Scarlett standing at the counter. I sit in the staff lounge and pull my phone out of my back pocket.

Me: I'm so sorry for this morning; I didn't know how Mrs Silver would react to us being together. I'm sorry James, please text or call me back. I hate not hearing from you.

I wait for a reply from James, but I know that I'm going to wait a very long time. He is gone. I can't bring myself to tell Scarlett that I won't be going to the party. She is so excited for me. I try on various outfits for her and in the end we settle on a not to dressy dress and heels, not too big though. I give her a satisfied look that shows her I'm happy with the outfit, even though I probably won't be going. We lock up the store and walk to our cars.

"I will meet you at home, okay?" I say before getting into my car. I check my phone again, but nothing. The drive home felt longer that it was. Scarlett is already in the house when I pull into our drive. I take a deep breath and climb out of the car. My phone pings, which lets me know that I have a text. I look at the screen. It's a text from James.

James: Is that what we are ....together?? You could have fooled me!!!

Tears spring to my eyes, I've really hurt him. I can't stop my stomach from painfully knotting up.

Me: I said I was sorry and I really am, please believe me. I miss you, can I see you tonight? Please James, we need to talk.

I hit send and sit and wait for his reply but after what seems like forever I give up and go inside. Scarlett is in the kitchen making us a bite to eat. "God Talls, what took you so long? I got here ages ago."

"Sorry Scar, I was on the phone to Bella from work. What are you cooking?" Smells like chicken stir fry.

"I'm going to have a quick shower before dinner, okay? I won't be long."

"You'd better not, Pup!" Scarlett shouts at me as I run up the stairs towards my bathroom. Turning the water on, I start to get undressed. My phone beeps and my heart skips a beat.

James: No! I can't tonight, I'm busy.

I sink into the chair in the bathroom feeling like I have yet again lost him. I type my reply.

Me: When can I see you? We need to talk James. Please.

I sit and wait again but give in, as I need to shower before Scarlett rips me a new one. The water is hot but it doesn't take my mind off James. I just stand under the water letting it run over my aching body but I can't cry not now. Scarlett is going to ask way too many questions and I'm just not in the mood for her twenty questions on my love life.

I climb out of the shower and make my way to my bedroom. I dry slowly and get dressed sluggishly, not really having the energy to do anything. I brush my hair and tie it back, not bothering to dry it. I'm not going back out tonight.

I meet my sister at the dining table, where my food is ready and waiting to be eaten. It smells delicious but I don't think my stomach can handle it. I will try for Scarlett though, since she already cooked and plated it.

"You okay, Talls? You're not looking right." She gives me a concerned look.

I smile and shrug, "I'm okay, just a busy day at work. It's coming to the end of the summer and everyone wants to get their family photos done and portfolios need to be updated. Things like that." I start to eat my food but struggle, thinking about James again. My stomach tightens again. Scarlett's phone rings, bring me back to the now. I hear her saying, "Okay" and "Will do" and she ends the call. "Who was that?"

"Just a friend," but she doesn't look up at me. I remember that I have left my phone in the bathroom, so I sprint up the stairs and check my phone. There is a text from James.

James: I really don't know. I have a busy week so....cya around.

He has really left me, and tears stream down my face and I can't breathe. How could he do this to me? He promised that he would never give up and told me 'he loved me'. I sink to the bathroom floor with a thud, pain shooting through my knees, but the pain of my breaking heart is much worse.

Chapter 14

I don't notice Scarlett joining me on the floor until she has her arms wrapped around me, rocking me back and forth. "Shhh Pup, it will be okay." I stop crying by her words and look up at her.

"I need to see him … tonight. I hurt him. I pulled away when Erica came into the studio. I didn't know how she would feel about us being together. We just got together and he walked away so easily," I try to lift myself up off the floor but Scarlett stops me, holding me to her.

"Pup leave him, he isn't worth it." I can hear the anger in her voice.

"But Scar…" She cuts me off.

"Natalia Slone, you will stay clear of him for a few days, okay? Promise me you will do that, give yourself some time?" Maybe she is right. I should cut him off like he has with me. Obviously I didn't mean that much to him. I nod but stand anyway.

"I'm going to bed Scar, I need to be alone right now." Scarlett leaves me in my room. I climb into bed and weep into my pillow, which still smells like James Wilde. I cry until my body gives in and falls asleep.

It's been two days since I saw James last. I distract myself by running myself ragged again. I wake to the sun shining through my window and my phone ringing, 'It's too early to be calling people!' I shout at my phone. "Hey Miss Tally, did I wake you?" Oh God, it's Carlos.

"Oh my God, am I late for work? Did I sleep through my alarm?" I sit upright and glance at the clock on my wall. It says it's five-fifteen. I relax and fall back down on my bed and I can hear Carlos laughing. "Yes Carlos, you woke me. What's up? Is everything okay?"

He stops laughing, "We have been given a permit to do a shoot on a location and it's your contract Talls, you need to get over there ASAP. Can you do that? I will email you the details, okay?" Without me answering, he ends the call. Great. I stagger out of bed and go shower. I quickly dry my body, still aching by the way, and get dressed.

Today I'm going for skinny jeans and my Exposure thick strap camisole and if Scarlett doesn't like it, then tough. I head to the kitchen and Scarlett is no-where to be found. Then I remember it's stupid o'clock, she won't be up yet. I scribble a note and head out to the location. Carlos has sent all my equipment over already, so they are just waiting on me. I have The Script playing in my car to calm my down, as there is a high possibility that Wilde is going to be there.

I turn down a tree lined lane and at the top on the road there is a stunning, larger than life house, no doubt worth millions. There are cars and trucks parked to the one side, so I park my Wrangler in the same place. I bang my head on the steering wheel and try to slow my breathing down. A tap on my window startles me; I whip my head around to see who it is. Staring at me is this petite young girl, with short designer blond hair and a huge smile across her face. I exit my car and she greets me with her chipper morning attitude.

"Morning Tally, I'm Cleo. I will be your PA while you're on this QBC contract. Everyone is inside waiting for you." I look at her as she hands me a thermal mug of tea.

"Morning Cleo, who is in there exactly?" She looks at me as if to say should-you-already-know-who-is-in-there.

"Um, Mr Williams, Miss Vogel and some guy called Marcus. I don't know what he does on the show, but he is hot." We walk towards the house and Cleo blurts out, "Oh, and Mr Wilde is here." I stop in my tracks and blink a few times trying to gather my thoughts.

"As in, James Wilde? He is here now?" She smiles and nods. I follow Cleo into the house, through the main hall and the kitchen. We reach the garden, where all my staff and equipment have already been set up. I can't see James, but Carmen is sitting by one of the patio tables. I make a bee line for Mr Williams. "Good morning Mr Williams. Sorry I'm late." He stands to greet me and offer his hand.

"It's perfectly fine Miss Slone; we weren't told until the early hours that we could use this magnificent home and garden."

I feel some tension leave my shoulders but its short lived when see Carmen darting towards me. Arms open, she pulls me in for a hug and kisses both my cheeks. "Oh Tally, it's so good to see you again. How is the job going? Good I hope." She has the most perfectly white teeth that I have ever seen before. I still don't get a good vibe from her.

"So this is the famous Tally Slone?" I hear a man say my name over my shoulder. I close my eyes briefly and turn to face the man. I know as soon as my eyes rest on his face that it's Marcus, but I don't give it away.

"And you are sir...?" I present my hand and he laughs, a full head back laugh.

"Like you don't know. I'm sure James has talked about me before today." I lower my hand and straighten my shoulders.

"And why would Mr Wilde be talking to me about you Mr? I still didn't catch your name."

He chuckles. "I'm Marcus Wright. James's best friend and bodyguard," he says, with a wicked grin on his lips. I steady my breathing, trying not to give away how irritated I'm feeling right now.

"Well, it's nice to meet you Mr Wright. Please, could you tell me where Mr Wilde is? I'm sure that everyone would like to get started now that I'm here." Marcus points to a tent down on the grounds. I thank him and walk towards the tent. Taking deep breaths, saying to myself,

'*Just breathe, you can do this Pup.*'

As I get closer to the tent, I can hear giggling and talking. It's James' voice and my breath catches again when I hear a girl's voice. Less than forty-eight hours and he has moved on from me. Wow, I was only fooling myself.

"Are you single James? Please tell me you are. I would love to taste your cock right now; I have heard so many stories about it." Fuck me, this girl has no shame!

Before James can answer her, I enter the tent. James is sitting in a high chair, and the make-up artist is standing between his legs, rubbing her hands up and down his thighs.

James must hear the tent door move, because without looking in my direction James speaks, "I will be out when I'm ready." I cross my arms over my body.

"Well, that will be a whole three minutes then won't it, Mr Wilde?" I smile to myself. I like this Tally. Wilde spins around and faces me.

"Tally, what are you doing here? I thought Sam was working today." I walk further into the tent and the make-up tart is blushing big time.

"You know this is my contract, or have you forgotten that? Since you have obviously forgotten a few other things too. Oh, by the way Mr Wilde, I believe this very young girl asked you a question. I think it's only polite on your part that you answer said question."

Make-up whore moves past me and exits the tent. "Oh, don't leave on my account. I believe that Mr Wilde wants you to finish working him over ... oh, I mean working on him!" I yell after her. James stands and shoves his hands in his jean pockets, and as he goes to speak I raise my hand to stop him.

"So much for not giving up on me. I can't believe I fell for it again." James' head whips up at me from the floor and he frowns.

"What the fuck is that supposed to mean?" He is pissed and I just chuckle to myself.

"You played me like Dean did, but without the rape and the beatings. You spent time with me, told me you understood everything that had happened. For fuck sake Wilde, you told me you loved me. I let my guard down and made love to you." I rub my eyes and look back at him, "No I fucked you, isn't that right Wilde? Then, after all that, I make one simple fucking mistake and you run. That was the perfect excuse for you to fuck and run. You are pathetic, Wilde. You know how hard it was for me to sleep with you? I deserve better."

We stand there staring at each other for the longest of times, waiting for the first move. It's James who takes the first steps. He moves closer to me and reaches for my face but I step back "Don't Wilde" He sighs.

"Please stop calling me Wilde. I like hearing you say my name."

"Wilde is your name, isn't it what your friends call you?"

He takes another step closer and again I move back. "You're my girlfriend and I love you calling me James. Please baby." I frown.

"Girlfriend? You could have fooled me," I say throwing his words back at him. He looks shocked by the tone in my voice.

"I just walked in on you and that slut. She was asking to give you a blowjob Jam..." I stop. I can't say him name. He runs a hand through his perfect hair. Oh, how I want to do that. Stay strong Natalia.

"I would have told her I had a girlfriend but you came in before I could say anything. Please believe me baby."

"I am not your baby," I growl at him. I catch my reflection in the mirror and make my way over to the table, walking straight past James, brushing my arm gently against his. I pull my hair tie out and start to brush my hair.

I can see James watching me. He stands there all sex-god like, with his hands stuffed in the back pockets of his jeans. I straighten my hair and decide to add some make-up as I didn't have time at home, thanks to Carlos. I roll on the mascara; add a thin line of eyeliner, and look around for the perfect lip gloss.

I add a natural pink to my lips, then smack them together and slowly run my tongue along them. I can see James licking his lips. Good, it's working. I smile, then bite my bottom lip. I stand there looking at myself in the mirror, thinking how much I have missed this Natalia Slone. I feel and look more confident.

James steps forward to me, slides his arms around my waist and lays light kisses on my neck. "You smell divine, baby. Can I kiss you, Tally?" I can feel his smile on my neck because he knows that was the same question he asked me the first time he kissed me.

"Not a good idea Wilde," I have to fight the shiver trying to run through my body.

"Oh for the love of God Natalia, call me James." I try to pull away but he tightens his hold on me.

"Fine, if I call you James will you let me go? I have work to do." I sigh "We have work to do." A wicked smile crosses his face.

"If you call me James and let me kiss you, I promise to let you get back to work." Oh, I have missed his kisses, even though it hasn't been that long since we actually kissed.

"I just think we should let this be and get back to work, okay? It's for the best, Wilde." He sounds angry again and steps back from me.

"My name is James, for fuck sake Tally. Is this how you want to end us?" I shake my head and laugh at him. I can't believe he wants to blame me for this.

"You blew me off, you're ending this not me. I told you over and over again that I was sorry for what I did, but can you blame me? I haven't worked for Exposure long and all of a sudden I'm fucking one of their biggest clients. I was going to tell Mrs Silver, but now I can see that I won't need to." I try walking away again but he grips my arm. He closes his eyes briefly and then looks down at me.

"Kiss me Tally, you know you want to." I sigh, feeling defeated.

"Fine! James, you can kiss me." I know I'm going to regret this kiss. A small but very sexy smile appears on his soft lickable lips. He pulls me tight to his body and I place my hands on his chest to keep a safe-ish distance.

"Don't fight me baby, please," James's lips brush mine softly at first, then he pulls back from me, then bring his lips back to mine once again. I'm in trouble now. My heart rate picks up speed and I know that I should stop this now before it gets too far. I pull away from James and put some distance between us.

"We have work to do James, we need to go." I turn to walk away but James wraps his arms around my waist and pulls me close to him. He brushes my hair to the one side and kisses my neck.

"I'm sorry Tally, I really am. I should have understood why you pulled away from me." I'm happy that he can now see why I did what I did, but his actions hurt just as much. "I'm not like Dean, you know that, babe. I never meant to hurt you, but fuck Tall you hurt me too … at the time, but I get why and I understand it. Please, can we just move on from this now?"

I pull out of James's hold and walk towards the tent door. I can feel James staring at me but I don't look back at him, but instead say, "We have work to do James, get a move on, yeah?" I can hear him sigh heavily and I feel a slight pang of guilt. "If we get this shoot done quickly enough, perhaps you can take me out dinner. You game?"

I wink at him and then I exit the tent, smiling to myself. I can give him another chance since it was both of us that screwed up this time. I start to climb the steps and I hear James running towards me, so I look over my shoulder and smile.

"You had better run baby, because I will catch you, and when I do this photo shoot will just have to wait." I squeal and start running towards everyone. I just get to the top step and James catches me by my waist and swings me around. I giggle out loud and everyone stops what they are doing and turn to face us. James turn me around to face him; he is wearing my favorite smile. His fuck-me smile.

"Where the fuck have you two been? Or shouldn't I ask?" A gruff voice comes from behind me. James breaks our gaze to look over my shoulder at Marcus.

I blush, even though I know we haven't done anything. "Just spending time with my girl, you got a problem with that dude?" I kiss James' jaw and pull away.

"Come on, we have work to do." I walk past Marcus, who puts his hand on my arm to stop me.

"It's nice to finally meet you, Tally." I smile and walk away to set up the first shots.

Chapter 15

During the photo shoot, James flirts with me every chance he gets, just the minor of touches, whispering in my ear. Every time I check the shot on my laptop, James has to stand behind me to check also. Marcus often passes comments at us, but I know he means well. Carmen isn't pleased with us, but hey, he is my boyfriend, not hers. Marcus doesn't leave my side and we chat throughout the day. He really is a nice guy. We chat about how long he has known James, what it was like growing up next to him.

Marcus sees James's parents as his own since his parents were killed a car accident when Marcus was twelve. Scarlett would love him and eat him alive. We get completely engrossed in the shoot. James is looking super hot in his show outfits. At the moment, he is wearing a light three-piece grey suit with a thin black tie and dress shoes.

Carmen is trying her hardest to get James to notice her more, but he seems to only have eyes for me, which makes me blush uncontrollably. This hot and sexy man has made love to me, put that sexy as sin mouth on me. I blush at the thought and bite my lip. I catch James looking at me. He tilts his head to one side and studies me. I send him a smile and he walks over to me and whispers in my ear.

"If you don't stop looking at me like that, we are going to have to abandon the shoot for an hour because I need to be deep inside you right now." A shiver escapes my body. James stiffens and grabs my hand. "Take an hour everyone. I need to sort a few things out with Miss Slone here." I blush all over because I know what everyone is thinking. Damn me for not being able to say no to James.

I can hear Marcus laughing behind me and shouting after James, "That's my boy!"

James pulls me along the trees and flower bed towards a small building at the bottom of the garden. It's a little outdoor guest house. It's decorated with bare brick walls and a complete glass roof. There is summer furniture in pastel colors. James takes me straight through to the bedroom.

He locks the door behind us and pins me to the door, crushing his lips to mine. I lick James's lips and he parts his mouth, letting my tongue dance with his. He still tastes so damn good. I run my fingers through his hair and tug slightly; a small groan comes from James throat.

"Bed, now." I say to James. He doesn't need to be told twice. He holds me by my ass cheeks and carries me over to the bed. Both of us fall onto the bed and James makes quick work of my clothes. I follow suit with his. James starts kissing my neck. He slowly runs his tongue down my neck and down across my collarbone, making his way to my breasts. He pulls my top up and my bra down. Flicking my nipple with his tongue making it hard and erect, he sucks hard, making me arch my back and cry out.

We strip each other of our clothes. He runs his hand slowly down my body and parts my legs. I'm breathing faster now. I just need to feel James inside of me, to feel him make my world explode. He slips a finger into me and I moan; I need more. He knows me because he slips in another and then another, while still sucking hard on my nipple. I feel that familiar feeling again and I know my orgasm is close.

"Faster James, please. I missed you. I need to come, James."

James's fingers pick up speed and I explode around him, trying to catch my breath. I feel James placing himself between my legs and he freezes.

"What's wrong babe?" I ask.

"Fuck, I don't have any condoms, baby. Shit. I'm gonna have to stop." He goes to pull away, but I place my hands on his firm ass and stop him.

"James I'm on the pill and you know I haven't been with anyone since Dean and I was tested after him. If you say you're clean, then I trust you." He leans back down to kiss me, sucking on my bottom lip.

"I'm clean baby, always use a condom. Never in all my life have I had sex without one." He kisses me. "Don't need Little Wilde's running around....yet." He smirks. I can feel him place himself at my opening, all slicked and wet from my orgasm. "Fuck Tally, you're so wet."

My body is aching more for him. "Please James, I need you inside me … now." With that James eases into me, slowly, inch by inch. I grab onto his ass and force him in deeper, but James holds his ground.

"You're killing me Tally, let's just take this slow. I haven't had you for what seems like years. I'm going to come so damn quick if we go fast."

I look into James's ocean blue eyes and cup his face with my hand, running my thumb over his bottom lip. "James, make love to me." He starts to move. I run my hands down his back, dragging my nails up and down his hard muscular back. James moans and picks up the pace.

"God, you feel so good baby. Fuck. You close baby? I'm going to come." Our breathing is fast and heavy. James brings his hand between us and starts rubbing my clit with his thumb. That was all it took. My body stars to tighten and pure bliss runs through my limbs as I cry out James's name.

"Harder, James…Harder." James pounds into me a few more times and he stills while his orgasm rips through his body

. James lowers his lips to mine and kisses me tenderly. He pulls back from me and I instantly miss his touch. James helps me off the bed and hands me my clothes. We get dressed in silence, but I can feel him staring at me.

Out of nowhere there is a loud bang on the door. "James, you finished yet dude? Carmen isn't impressed by you taking off with Tally. She is pissed man. You two need to get back to work and get this shoot finished, you have a meeting after this." Marcus shouts through the door. Fuck. I had forgotten about the photo shoot. Damn James and his mind blowing sex.

We finish getting dressed and exit the guest house to find Marcus leaning against a tree. I smile at him and he just shakes his head and laughs to himself. "You need to be prepared for Carmen man, she is on a rampage that you left her there." James laughs.

"Fuck her man, I needed time alone with my girl and did you see the faces she was giving. Fuck me faces, is that right baby?" He says as he pulls me tight to his side and kisses my hair.

I put my hands over my face and let out a little laugh. "Not fuck me faces Wilde, they were me remembering what you feel like inside me, and your mouth on me." I smirk and wink at Marcus who is looking at me with wide shocked eyes. I turn to James and he pretty much has the same expression on his face.

"What? You didn't think that I could say things like that in front of Marcus, that I would just blush and shy away. Oh baby, I can handle myself around guys like you two. I know how you work. You haven't met my brother Jake yet or any of his team. I grew up with horny ass teenage soccer players." I shrug and walk away, leaving the two speechless hotties behind me.

I get back to my table where my laptop is set up and start flicking through the photos. The staff are mulling around drinking coffee and eating from the buffet. This is how I like to work, cool, calm and collected. There is no need for drama. Speaking of drama, Carmen comes storming towards me with a not so happy look on her face.

"Where the fuck did you vanish to? I have a very, very important meeting to get to and I don't appreciate you running off to fuck my co-star. That is very unprofessional of you. I will be having a word with Erica about this." She has gone all red in the face and me, well I have lost all color.

"He isn't just some co-star Carmen, he is your friend, and by the way, my boyfriend. Yes we shouldn't have left the shoot, but honestly, did it look like I could stop him? Would you have stopped him?" Everyone is standing around watching us argue, well Carmen arguing and me making a point. When she doesn't say anything I keep going.

"Yeah. That's what I thought Carmen. You don't say no to James Wilde and believe me doll, I don't ever intend to." She scowls at me and storms right back the way she came.

I turn to see James and Marcus clapping their hands in sync. "Well said sweetness, it's about time someone set her straight and told her to shut the fuck up," said Marcus with a huge grin on his beautiful face. Oh yes, Scarlett is going to love him.

We wrap up the shoot. Cleo and I are packing the equipment away in the two trucks they arrived in. Carmen is long gone, which pleases me in a big way. I watch James and Marcus walk towards my car as I make my way over. "So, will I see you tonight, or will your meeting be a long one?" He places his hand on my hips and kisses me.

"I will pop by after the meeting, it won't take long. It's just a chat about the wrap party and the publicity that we have to do for the show." I nod my head.

"Okay babe, I will see you later then. I need to get this back to Exposure and I will start going over the photos from today. Scarlett is working and I don't fancy sitting by myself at home." James kisses me again and pulls away.

"Well, text me when you're leaving Exposure and I will let you know where I am, okay? Perhaps you can pick me up on your way home."

I nod. "Okay, sounds like a plan." He opens my car door for me and I climb in and smile at him.

"Baby, I'm taking you shopping for a new car sometime soon. I hate you driving around in this contraption." I feel my eyebrows hit my hairline.

"Excuse me? You're what?" He just shrugs.

"You need a new car babe. This thing isn't safe." I laugh, closing the door and starting my jeep.

"My car is perfect, James. I don't need you to buy me a new car. If I want a new car, I will buy one myself. Also, for your information James Wilde,"

I lower my voice and crook my finger at him to come closer. "I'm worth more than you, Mr. Wilde. My bank balance has way more than you. So you see, I don't need you to buy me a car. I can do that perfectly on my own. You get me?"

James is gobsmacked once again. Yay me. That's twice in one day I have rendered James silent and it feels good. Not so smooth now is he? I didn't lie to James, as everything I just told him is true. Scarlett, Jake and myself are trust fun babies, but we all used our money differently when we had our instalments

126

I drive back to Exposure and help unload all the equipment with Cleo and the guys. Once that's done, I head back to my studio and upload the photos from today's shoot to the company server so that Erica can take a peek when she is ready.

I sort through all the photos and send my choice over to Erica and Mr. Williams; it doesn't take up too much of my afternoon. I glance at my phone and it's been two hours since I left the shoot. I haven't heard anything from James, his meeting must be important. I decide to take a sneak peek into the Google life of James Wilde. I search his name and click on the images that they have of him.

My stomach sinks like a lead balloon. There are photos of James with different women; they are all drop dead gorgeous. Why does he like me when he can have all these women? I don't understand it. I feel sick. Oh God, what if I'm just filling in until he finds someone he really wants? I know he told me he loves me, but how many women has he told he loves them?

I decide to get off the images and click on news feeds of James. There are dated events that he has appeared at, red carpet type events, also charity galas. Nate comes to mind and a small smile creeps on my face.

I see that a link has been posted with today's date and I wonder if that has something to do with the photo shoot. That would be good for the company of the name is mentioned. The website loads up and there is a headline that reads.

"James Wilde back with ex-girlfriend, movie star, Sasha Davenport? Both seen leaving restaurant down town earlier this afternoon."

There is a stream of photos of James a very beautiful woman leaving the restaurant and hugging at the side walk. In the next photo, they are kissing full on mouth and then they are both sitting in the back of the car really close. I feel tears spring to my eyes and I can't breathe.

It was all a lie.

Chapter 16

I don't remember leaving the studio or driving to Cassidy's apartment. Everything is just one teary blur. Why did he do this to me? I walk into Cass and Josh's apartment and find Cassidy sitting on the couch and Josh on his laptop. They both look up at me as I drop my bag on the floor. I feel strong arms around and pick me up. From the smell, I know its Josh that has caught me from falling to the floor.

"Oh my God Tally, what the hell has happened?" says Cassidy. I shake my head, unable to speak. I have to show them. I can't talk right now. I point to the laptop and I see Josh frowning but he hands it to me. I type in the website and show them. I hear Cassidy gasp and Josh swear under his breath.

"I'll fucking kill him. What the fuck is he playing at?" I swallow the huge lump in my throat.

"We made up this morning, we talked at the photo shoot and we made love." I stop myself "No he fucked me. He told me he had a meeting about the wrap party and he wouldn't be long. I know it's only been two, well nearly three hours now, but I haven't heard from him, and that's why." I say pointing towards the laptop, anger bursting out of me.

"Cassidy I love him. I don't know if I can survive this." She hugs me closer and rocks back and forth, as she knows that's what sooths me. I hear my phone ring and I feel sick all over again. Josh brings me my bag and I dig out my phone.

"You don't have to talk to him Tal." I look over at Josh.

"I do Josh. I need to tell him it's over. We are done."

I get up and walk towards their guest room, which sometimes morphs into my room. I take a deep breath and answer my phone. "Hello?" I say weakly.

"Baby I'm just finishing up and then I can meet you at your place. That sound good for you?" Tears start to flow again.

"James, I don't think it's a good idea anymore." I wipe the tears away, but more keep falling.

"What's not a good idea? Baby, you're scaring me. What's happened? Has Carmen done something after what happened at the shoot today?"

"No. Carmen hasn't hurt me James, you have. Listen it's..." I don't finish what I'm going to say as James cuts me off.

"What the fuck? How have I hurt you Tally? I haven't done anything. When I left you at the shoot, we were happy. I came to the restaurant had my meeting. We ate, and now I'm on the phone with my girlfriend, who is breaking up with me for fuck knows what reason. Tell me what I have supposedly done, Natalia." Fuck, he used my full name, just like Scarlett. He sounds pissed, not that he has any right to be. I'm fighting the sobs that are threatening to break through.

"Sasha." That's all I say. I hear James take in a quick breath and mutter 'Fuck', but he doesn't say anything else.

God, I was so damn stupid. I knew it was too good to be true. Guys like James Wilde don't fall for plain Jane's like me.

"That's what I thought. Good bye, James. Please don't contact me again."

Before he can say anything, I hang up. I drop my phone on the floor and curl up in a protective ball on the bed. I hear the door open and Cassidy climbs into the bed with me. She is spooning me from behind. She is my absolute rock, always has been. I feel the bed dip again and I open my eyes to see Josh climbing into the bed in front of me.

He wraps his arms over the both of us and we just lay there in complete silence. My phone rings and rings and then the texts start. I can't even think about him right now. I hear Cassidy's gentle snores and I let a smile slip across my face. I look at my best friend's boyfriend, who is watching me.

"Hi." He gives me my Joshy smile.

"Hi Pup, you okay?" Josh started calling me Pup after he got introduced to Scarlett and Jake; it stuck with him after that day.

"I will be Josh, I promise. I just thought that after everything with Dean, I thought I would never find someone, you know." He nods, he gets me. "I let him in, Josh. I never thought I would be able to do that again, and then he does this. Fuck, I hate men." He pulls his head back and cocks his eyebrow; I giggle.

"Present Company excluded. You're a star, Josh, and I love you for that. The way you take care of Cassidy and me when needed. You're the other big brother I always wanted." I hug him tighter. My phone rings again and Josh leans over the bed to pick it up. He glances at the screen.

"There are fifteen missed calls from James, Pup, six from Scarlett. I think you need to text her and let her know you're okay. You know how she worries." I nod and take my phone. I swipe the lock bar and dial Scarlett's number.

131

"Hi, I'm okay Scarlett. No I'm with Cass and Josh right now. Scar don't you dare tell him where I am! No, just leave it!" I sit up. "You're MY sister, you don't owe him shit. Just tell him to stop calling me. I will explain later okay? Oh yeah, and what did he have to say about that?" I shake my head and take a deep breath. "Fine whatever, tell him I will be there in twenty minutes. Don't let him in the house Scar, I mean it. Okay, bye." I climb over Josh and stand, looking down at him and a now awake Cassidy.

"Do you want us to come with you, babe?" I bite my lip thinking about what to do.

"No Cass, it's fine babe. If Josh gets within two feet of James, I think he will beat the shit out of him." We all laugh.

Josh looks at me "What did he tell Scar?"

"He told her that she was there in the meeting with them, as she is organising a charity gala in December that's linked to James's charity for Nate. They thought the meeting would kill two birds with one stone, but little does James know that he has killed three birds." I shrug.

"Listen, I had better go. I will let you know how it all goes, okay? I love you guys to the moon and back." They both jump off the bed and hug me tight, reining kisses all over my face and head. I smile into Josh's chest.

"We love you too Pup." I groan and they laugh again.

I think about James and Sasha on my drive home. I can't help but wonder what lame ass excuse he is going to use as to why they kissed and snuggled in the back of the cab. He thinks he is so smooth. We shall see what he has to say for himself. Twenty minutes later, I pull into the drive at my house and see James leaning against his car, looking sexy as sin.

He has his head down, arms crossed across his chest, legs are crossed at his ankles. Goddamn it, why did he have to look so good all the time? I can feel myself softening towards him already just from his looks. Fuck, I need to stay strong. James sees my car and pushes off his BMW, but doesn't make a move towards me. I take a few calming breaths before exiting my car. I climb out and straighten my shoulders and walk towards him and greet him. "Hi."

"So without any explanation from me you cut me off, shut me out? Do I mean that little to you Tally?" Wow wasn't expecting that, but then again I don't know what I was expecting.

"Wow. Typical guy move, blame the so-called only girl in your life. Nice move, Wilde." I go to step around him, but he grabs me by my arm.

"I think we need to talk about this Tally." I jerk my arm back and look him in the eyes.

"You kissed another woman, and not just any woman Wilde, your ex-girlfriend of all people." I can tell by his expression that he is pissed that I'm back to calling him Wilde, which I know he hates.

"I didn't kiss another woman Tally, she kissed me. It was a friendly kiss on the lips, it's what we do. We have known each other a very long time baby. Sasha is getting married next summer and she has just found out she is pregnant and is unsure as to what Chad will say." I stand there staring at him, not knowing what to say. The passenger door on James's car opens and I'm shocked as to who steps out. Sasha comes around the car and stands next to James.

She smiles a warm smile at me. "Hi Tally I'm Sasha, but I guess you already know who I am." I nod and look at James. Why the hell has he brought her here?

"I don't get why you're here Sasha. I really don't want to sound like a total bitch, but I think you two should both leave. I need time to think and I can't do with you two here, knowing you shared a kiss, and God knows what else this afternoon." I walk away and almost make it to my front door. James catches me by the elbow.

"Oh, for fuck sake, Tally. Did you not hear what I just told you? We are just friends. Is this your way out? Of not letting me in fully and letting Dean win again? He gets your heart, but I don't? He got to love you and do all that you to and you stayed." I whip my head to look at him, fresh tears leaking down my face.

"Oh fuck baby, I didn't mean that. Shit, I'm so sorry Tally, baby please." He reaches for me again and I step back, still locking eyes with him. I can see the sadness and regret in his eyes, it's all over his face. I turn to see Sasha with her hand over her mouth, tears slowly making their way down her cheeks. Oh my God, he told her.

"Do you know how hard it was for me to see the headlines and all those pictures of you and Sasha kissing and hugging in the back of a cab?" He doesn't speak. "Well do you James?"

He shakes his head no. "No? Well I'll tell you now Wilde, it fucking hurts? It ripped me in two. After everything that went down with Dean, I really thought that we would work out, but I don't know if I can do this James. Tell me what you would do if you saw me kissing Dean or another guy that I dated before you. So much has happened in the last few days, and it's too much for me to deal with. My head is all over the place." His head shoots up to mine and he looks scared.

"You're leaving me?" I look away from the sadness in his eyes.

"Maybe it's for the best James. You can do so much better than a fucked up girl like me. Just please don't make this any harder than it already is." I look down at Sasha, who is now at the bottom of the porch steps.

"Tally please don't do this. James and I have had a connection for years, as I had a brother who died just like Nate, that's how we know each other. We will always be friends, closer than most friends yes, because we dated for a while. But for the past two years, we have been nothing more than friends. I'm happy with Chad and I'm looking forward to our future together, but James needs you Tally, he has completely changed since he met you." I look at James. He has tears in his eyes and it breaks my heart. She keeps going as me and James just stare at each other.

"He phoned me the night after you two met. He told me he danced with this amazing girl. He was still a little drunk because he kept going on about how she smelt and tasted like pineapple." Still looking at each other, a smile creeps across our faces.

"Is that what you meant when you told me the day of my interview that you enjoyed the view?" His smile gets bigger.

"Yeah baby, we danced for a few songs. You where grinding on me, had your arms around my neck. Fuck you smelt so damn good. I had to have a taste so I did." He shrugs as if it's nothing.

"A taste? I don't remember kissing you, or anyone that night." I scratch my head "Actually I don't remember much about that night at all." A little laugh escapes me.

"I was kissing your neck, but you starting moaning and your friends pulled you away. I so would have taken you home that night and never let you go."

A black town car pulls up in front of my house and both James and I turn to it. Sasha is smiling at us both. She places her hands on both sides of my face. "Tally, let him in. He loves you. He is just too damn stubborn to say it. You are good for each other. Stick with it Tally." I smile at her and she turns to James with a bigger smile on her face.

"You, my boy, need to tell your girl how you feel. It's evident how she feels for you. Nate would want you to find love and make a family of your own. 'Live and Breathe' James, remember that." She says has she places her hand over his tattoo on his ribs. More tears spring to my eyes as we watch Sasha climb into her car and drive away. I look back to James, who is staring at me again.

"So where do we go from here?" I say, looking him dead in the eyes.

 "I think we need to go inside and talk about us Tally. I get that you were upset and I'm so damn sorry that you had to see that but..." I turn and walk inside my house. I hear James walk behind me and close the door.

Chapter 17

"Would you like a drink or anything?" James shakes his head no. "Ok, well I'm going to have a beer. Why don't you have a seat in the living room?" I see flashes cross his face like he is figuring something out for the first time.

James just stands there. "Can we just talk this out please, because I'm getting the vibe that you're going to end us tonight. And to be honest Tally..." He trails off and rubs his hands over his face, he must see the uncertainty on my face. He thinks for a long time. I can almost hear the gears turning in his head. He is having second thoughts. I can see his face is pained, just like mine.

"Listen. I get it okay, this life isn't for everyone. Some people can handle being in the spot light and others can't and believe me bab..." he stops himself from calling me baby and I feel it like a knife to my heart. "Believe me when I say I understand that you can't do this. It will kill me to walk away, but I will because that's what you want." I knew this was coming. I place my unopened bottle on the kitchen counter and sag against it, praying my legs keep me upright. It's hard, as James is walking away. I blink away the tears trying to find my voice. He isn't fighting for us, but neither am I.

Perhaps this isn't meant to be.

My voice is still stuck in my throat as James makes his way over to me. My body stiffens and he places his hands on either side of my face

"I get it okay babe, believe me I get it. You will always own a piece of me Natalia Slone, always."

Tears fall down my cheeks, but James wipes them away with his thumbs. I can't take my eyes off of him. Why can't I tell him how I feel? Damn it

"One day I hope that you love someone enough to let them in. I had just hoped that, that someone would have been me." With that, he kisses my lips gently and pulls away. I'm still frozen in place while I watch him walk towards the door. He stops half way through the door and turns to me, it's then that I see the wetness on his cheeks. James is crying. "What Sasha said was right." He catches his breath.

"I love you Tally, I always will." He turns and leaves.

My legs give away and I crumble to the floor, sobbing my heart out. My heart just walked out the door and I did nothing to stop him. I rock back and forth, cradling my knees to my chest. Nothing will stop this pain I'm feeling, nothing. I have thrown away the best thing that has ever happen to me. I don't know how long I cry for, my eyes and throat is sore from all the sobbing. I pick myself up and make my way upstairs. I stand in my room, looking at the bed that I made love to James in a few days ago.

Fresh sobs erupt from me, when I hear the front door open. I quickly strip off my clothes and get into the shower, not caring that the water is always cold at first. I'm too numb to feel anything. I get myself under control and stand under the now high temperature water. After a few minutes, I hear the door creak open and Scarlett's voice rings out. "Pup you okay? How did things go with James?"

I steady my breath "Scar, can we not talk about this right now, please? I really just need to be alone right now, okay?"

I hear her sigh. "Okay, I'll be downstairs if you need me."

"I'm just going to go to bed when I get out. It's my day off tomorrow, so I'm going to go shopping and keep busy."

"So are you still wearing the dress to the wrap party?" I fight more tears.

"I'm not going, Scar. Let's just leave it at that please." I say wiping the tears away.

"Okay Pup, I will leave you alone for now, but remember this. You're my baby sister and if you're hurt, then I'm hurt. You will tell me what has happened with James." Just at the sound of his name, sobs breaks loose. "Shit Tally, what happened?" I turn the water off and step out. Scarlett, the best sister in the world, is standing there with a big white fluffy towel waiting for me. She wraps it around me and pulls me towards my room.

I'm standing in my bedroom while my sister wipes me down after my shower. God, I love her. She dresses me in my nightwear and helps me into bed. I'm lying in my bed, when Scarlett comes back into the room with her phone to her ear. "Okay cool, we will see you in a bit." I frown

"Who was that?" Oh God, please don't tell me it was James.

"Just Jake. He is going to bring some comfort food and we are all going to snuggle up and watch a movie, okay?" I nod and sit up.

"Did you tell Jake about James?" She shakes her head.

"I just told him what I know, that James cheated on you and it's over now." I gasp.

"Oh God Scar, James didn't cheat. James and Sasha explained it all to me. He left me because he thinks I can't handle the spot light. He left me because he thinks it's what I wanted. He thinks that I can't let him in after everything that happened with Dean. He told me he loves me Scarlett, and I let him walk away." I feel a tear hit my hand.

"You love him, don't you Pup?" I nod yes.

"It's too late now. He walked away Scar and I can't go to him after that, I just can't. If he isn't willing to fight for me, then what's the point in trying?"

"But Tally, you didn't fight for him either. You let him walk. You can't put all the blame on him. I bet you all of my trust fund that if you phoned him right now and asked to come back here, he would." I shake my head at her, knowing that from the look in his eyes he was done with me, with us.

"He wouldn't Scar, you didn't see his face before he left me. He is done." We sit in silence until I hear my big brother's voice break through the house.

"Yo ladies, where you at?" I can't help but laugh at Jake. My big brother rocks.

"We are up here Jakey!" I shout. I hear Jake take stomp up the stairs. He struts into my room and frowns when he sees me.

"Oh fuck no. He hurt you Pup? Don't lie to me, I will kick his fucking ass for you." I give him a small smile.

"He didn't hurt me Jake, calm down. Well, not physically anyway." I look down at my ring and start to twist it around on my finger. "He left me Jake, he walked away." I shake my head as James's face flashes in my head and I rub my chest. Jake sits on the bed next to me, pulls me into his side, and hugs me tight. He kisses the top of my head and a sob sneaks out.

"Shh Pup we are here. He won't hurt you again." He rocks me back and forth.

We all snuggle down to watch Fast Five. Yummy, Paul Walker.

Just seeing him on the screen hurts my chest, he reminds me of James. His hair, his smile. I miss him. My phone pings, alerting me of a text. Scarlett passes it over to me and Jake tries to look at whose name is on the screen.

"Hey nosey parker, get out of it." I laugh, looking down at my phone to see the text is from Cassidy.

Cassidy: Babe what happened? Why haven't you texted?

Me: Long story short, James left me. We are done. I love him, but it's too late.

Cassidy: WHAT?!!!!! Did u tell him?

Me: No, Cass just leave it. I will text tomorrow. Night.

Cassidy: Okay babe. Love you.

Me: Love you 2

I smile at my phone, turn it off, and snuggle back into Jake. I'm so lucky to have him for a big brother. I remember when he found Dean a few days after he was released from the police station. He beat Dean to a pulp. Now Jake is not a violent person, but Dean hurt his family and that's like hurting him. Dean didn't press charges, he just told the police that he was mugged. I don't know why he did it.

I thought he would have jumped at the chance to take Jake down, but he didn't. I am grateful for that because if Dean had pressed charges, Jake would have been fired from his soccer team and that team is his life. He sees those boys as his brothers; they all look out for each other. I remember not long after the Dean incident I went out with Cassidy, Josh, and everyone and got extremely drunk.

I was so drunk that I blacked out. I woke up the next day in a room that I didn't know. I remember walking out of the room, luckily still fully dressed, to find a really freaking hot guy sitting by a table in the kitchen. It turned out to be one of Jake's team mates who saw the state I was in and brought me home. I slept in his guest room, as Jake was away on vacation with a girl at the time. He was so sweet. He made me breakfast and then drove me home. We have stayed in touch from that night. He is like another big brother, just freaking hot.

I woke in my bed alone with the sun streaming through my bedroom window. I stretch and let out a groan. I lay there with a blank mind until the memories from last night come flooding back. I take a deep breath and make my way to my bathroom to have a hot shower. The water washes away my aches, but not my heart ache or my memories. I get dressed in shorts and a concert tee and blow dry my hair, leaving it down with its natural wave to it. I make my way downstairs to find my sister and brother eating breakfast.

They both look up when they hear me enter the kitchen. "Morning." I say, kissing Scarlett on the cheek and Jake on the top of his head.

"Morning Pup, how you feeling?" I shrug and open the fridge. I need OJ.

"I'm fine Scar. It will take time to heal, but I will get there." I say, pouring my drink. They look at each other and then back to me. "What? Listen it happened, get over it. He didn't want it enough to fight. And yeah I know it goes both ways. I'm hurt just as much as he is, but HE walked away, not me." I leave them and go and sit on my front porch. I need some fresh air.

I sit and watch the boys in the street play baseball. God, I would give anything to be that age again. Seth sees me and comes running across the street to see me. "Morning Miss Tally. Are you and James going to come and play a game with us today?" There is that pain again. I give him a weak smile.

"No, sorry Seth. James won't be coming around anymore, okay? Sorry buddy." His smile fades and he just nods and walks away. Why am I always hurting people? My phone beeps and I know by the noise that it's my calendar reminding me to book my hair appointment for the wrap party in a few days. I know that Scarlett will be disappointed that her clothes won't be on show there, but I also know that she understands that I can't go now. I make my way back into the house as Scarlett and Jake come out.

"I'm off to work, you going to be okay today? I don't have to go in." I shake my head.

"It's fine. Like I said last night, I'm going to go shopping and spend some cash I think." She smiles at me and kisses me on the cheek.
"Later, Pup." She waves and drives off. Jake and I stand there watching her drive away. I turn to look at my brother.

"So are you really okay, or are you just hiding it?" I shrug

"Haven't you got training to get to?"

"Yep, these morning sessions are a killer, man." He kisses the top of my head and heads to his car. "I'm here if you need anything Tally."

"I know Jakey, I know. Hey, say hi to Charlie for me, will you?" He nods and waves as he drives away.

I arrive at the mall and start wandering around. There isn't really anything I need, to be honest. I just didn't want to sit at home alone with me and my thoughts. I hit a very expensive lingerie store to buy some sexy nightwear. It's not like anyone will see it though, but it might make me feel better and sexier

. I wander around more stores, not buying much. I see a crowd of people just a few stores down, so I walk down to see what all the fuss is about. As I head down, the girl's giggles and chatter get louder. It must be a celebrity or something. I head closer and the flashes start going off, so yep it's a celeb. I manage to get closer by nudging my way through the crowd of girls, only to come face to face with James.

I freeze and I can feel my body go cold. He is talking to a guy with a TV camera and a microphone. He looks as if he is doing an interview. I can't move, so I have no choice but to listen.

"So, James, what was is like filming with such big names on Control?" James doesn't hesitate with his answer.

"It was amazing, like a dream come true." He smiles his mega-watt-smile and looks out to the crowd.

"It's rumoured that you and your co-star Carmen Vogel had an off screen affair, is that true?"

James laughs "Nope, we have never had any kind of romantic affair off screen."

"So is there anyone special waiting for you at home?" His face falls, but he recovers just as quickly as it falls.

"No Mike, no-one special. Well at least not at the moment. I'm happy being sing-" His eyes make contact with mine and he freezes mid sentence.

My body comes undone. I nod my head in understanding and bite my lip to stop the sob escaping, but not the tears. While turning and pushing my way back through the crowd, I hear my name.

"Tally, wait!" I don't listen. I head out to my Jeep as fast as I my feet will carry me.

Chapter 18

I make it to my car and throw my store bags into the back seat. I hear him again "Please baby, wait." I stop and turn to him, my anger boiling my blood.

"Baby? Baby? Really, Wilde? You think you have the right to call me that anymore? I'm just another conquest to you. What was it you said? There's no-one special waiting for you and you're happy being single right now? Well you're right, Wilde. I'm nothing special, and to be honest I should have known that I meant nothing to you. That you were just looking for a way out after I told you everything about Dean. I just can't believe that you would turn it around on me." The tears are flowing down my cheeks and my fists are clenched so tight I think I might have broken the skin. I see hurt cross his face and he shakes his head.

"I was never looking for an out, Tally. I love you. I think I always have since that first night we met. I could still smell you on me days later, no matter how many times I showered. Every time I smell pineapples I think of you. You are under my skin Natalia. It's just you refuse to let me love you. Dean has fucked you up so bad that he has ruined all men for you. I now have to live my life knowing that I wasn't enough for you, that you will never love me enough to let me love you." My breathe hitches.

"You're right James, Dean has ruined all men for me, but not in a good way. He raped me and beat me and threatened to kill my family. How do you think someone is supposed to get over that? Huh? By falling in love with a Hollywood star that could just as easy drop her like he did? I knew a life with you was going to be an emotional rollercoaster. You didn't fight for me James, for us. So that just showed me that you don't love me enough to let me love you."

I turn to open my car door when I hear him whisper.

"You love me?"

I climb into my Jeep and turn to James, who is standing in the parking lot staring at me, eyes locked on mine. "Yes James I love you, but it doesn't matter anymore does it?" I close my door and drive away, I watch James stand there, watching me drive away. My heart breaks all over again, shattering into a million pieces. I don't know if I can ever put my heart back together.

I turn the radio on and Ne-Yo's 'Let Me Love You' is playing. I listen to the lyrics and it's like James is singing to me. The words in the song cut me deep. I can feel every word that is being sung. It's our song, it describes everything in us. It's true, I have never felt a love like James's before. He can show me, he can love me. I have to pull over and try to catch my breath. I take deep breaths and slow my breathing down. I brush away my tears and think about everything that has happened in the short time I have known James Wilde. The first time I saw him on the laptop in Scarlett Avenue, the first time he touched me in JAG. All the memories come flooding back. In such a short time, James has buried himself in me, in my heart and my soul.

He takes the hurt away from my past.

I arrive home and head straight to my room. I climb into bed and pull the cover up over my head. All thoughts shift through my head again. I need to get a grip and sort my shit out. Dean pops into my head. That rat bastard has ruined me just like James said. He is totally to blame for all this. I need to see him. I reach for my phone on my bedside table and scroll through my contact list, praying that he hasn't changed his number. I find his name and hit the call button. He picks after a few rings. "Tally?"

"Dean, I know I'm the last person you want to talk to, but you owe me." He doesn't say anything, but I can hear him breathing.

"I never thought I would hear from you again after what I did to you. Tally you need..." I cut him off.

"Dean, will you meet me for a coffee, like today or tomorrow please? We need to sit down and talk."

He sighs. "Yeah babe. Shit, sorry Tally I didn't mean to call you that. It's just habit when I talk to you. I can meet now if you want?" I close my eyes at the thought of seeing him again, but I know it has to be done.

"Okay, I will meet you at Starbucks in say thirty minutes?"

"Sure Tally, see you soon." I hang up and hide back under the covers. After a few minutes, I swing my legs over the edge of the bed. I stand up just a little too fast and become dizzy. "Whoa." I sit back down onto my bed and wait for the room to stop spinning.

Once the room stops spinning, I stand slower this time. I make my way down the stairs and head out the door. I feel sick to my stomach the entire drive to meet Dean. I haven't seen him since that night. Will he be sorry for what he did? Will he bring up everything that he did?

A few minutes later, I pull into a parking space and walk down the meet him. I stop outside and see Dean Riley sitting there, staring at his hands. God, he still looks amazing, his dark blonde hair cut shorter that what it was. He still wore his shirts with the sleeves rolled up above the elbow.

I take a deep breath and make my way in. Dean's head snaps up as the bell above the door rings out. A small smile stretches across his face and he stands to greet me. I'm silently praying in my head that he doesn't hug me. I walk closer and notice that he has a new tattoo on the inside of his right wrist, it's a word but I can't quite work it out. I stop in front of him.

"Hi, Dean." I say, taking my seat.

"Hi Tally. Stupid question, but how have you been?" Deans asks shyly.

I shrug. "I have been okay, healing inside and out, you know. I haven't fully healed Dean, that's why I have asked you to meet me here. I need answers. I don't want to live with this hate anymore." I lay it all out there for him before he can speak. I'm too scared to hear his excuses right at the second, he needs to hear me first.

"It's taken me years to get over what you did to me, Dean. I couldn't bear the thought of anyone touching me that wasn't my parents, Scarlett, or Jake. Even Josh, Lucas couldn't touch me without me freaking out."

Guilt spreads across his face and he looks down at his hands on the table. I don't give him a chance to chime in. "You broke me Dean, you had ruined me for all other men, and I couldn't trust men at all. Over time I was able to let Josh and Lucas hug me and give me sweet brotherly kisses." I smile remembering my boys.

"I met Carly. Nice girl, Dean." I chuckle and he lifts his head to me with a small smile on his lips.

"Yeah, she told me. She was all wrong for me Tally. We are no longer together. She was seeing a friend of mine behind my back. Karma I guess, huh? I knew that we wouldn't last, she just wasn't for me. I threw away the only good person for me, I hurt her." My stomach knots and tears fill my eyes.

"What happened Dean?" I lower my voice "What made you hit me, rape me. You say I was the best for you, but you hurt me in the worse way. Then you brought Dylan and Evan home and look at what happened." So much for not bring up old memories.

"Tally, I will never forgive myself for hurting you the way I did. I was drinking and gambling and my life was going down the shit hole. I know it's no excuse, but I took it out on you and I shouldn't have. It was my dad's idea to cover it all up. I haven't told anyone the full details because when I got out of rehab I was too ashamed of what I had done." He looks out the window, avoiding my eyes. Fuck, Dean went to rehab? I didn't know this.

"Dean, when did you go into rehab?" He looks back to me.

"As soon as I was out of hospital after my…mugging." He shrugs.

"Is that why you didn't tell the police that Jake beat you up?" He nods and takes a sip of his coffee. I follow suit. I can't believe all this. "Are you better now? Are you seeing anyone new now that Freaky Carly is gone?" I smile at him and he returns the smile.

"Nope, I guess I'm just concentrating on me at the moment." I can't believe that I am here drinking coffee with Dean Riley after everything he put me through. He seems full of remorse for what he did to me. I can see in his eyes that he is truly sorry for what he did. I can also see that he won't be forgiving himself anytime soon; he is still fighting those demons.

"Are you still seeing that TV star that Carly told me about? What's his name, Jason something?" I laugh at his attempt.

I shake my head. "No Dean, his name is James Wilde. He is in the soon-to-be new show on QBC called 'Control'. No Dean, we are no longer together. I know that me saying this is going to hurt you, but it's because of you. He told me he loved me. I think I was just too guarded for him, but also, he couldn't fully get past what had happened with you and me. Neither of us fought for each other." I draw patterns on the table with my finger. Dean reaches over the table to touch my hand, but I flinch away. I see the guilt flash across his face.

"I can't Dean. You lost the right to touch me the first time you hit me, but you took it anyway." He looks away, finding it hard to look me in the eye. He takes a deep breath.

"Tally you can't let what I did to you ruin your relationship with this guy. You need to move on one hundred percent. I know what I did to you hurt in the worst possible way, but you need to move past me. Do you love him?" I nod and picture James lying in my bed playing with my hair. I smile to myself.

"Good honey, you need to love again. I think this Wilde dude will be good for you. Listen, I have to get to back to work. Dad is handing over some accounts to me. He is looking at slowing down, if you can believe that. Can I ring or text you? I should never be asking this, but can we keep in touch? I still love you Tally, and I always will, but I need you to understand that you need to move on from me."

I nod and look at his wrist his tattoo, which now I can see. "Forgive" I smile up at him.

"I forgive you Dean, I hope you know that. I didn't think I could, but seeing you here, it's changed how I feel about you some. I'm not sure if it's a good idea for us to keep in touch. Like you said, you need to concentrate on you Dean and having me ring or text you will bring up memories that we both need to forget and move forward from." We both stand and head for the door. Once we are outside we stand there face to face, not saying anything.

"Well Tally, you look good and I'm happy that you are happy. You need to go get this guy back. You love him and he loves you, so don't let it go honey, don't throw it away like I did, okay? You will regret it, Miss Natalia Slone." I let out a little laugh

"I will try my very best, Mr. Dean Austin Riley. Will you be okay?" He nods.

"Can I hug you Tally? I know it's a lot to ask, but this just seems like a final goodbye." I bite my lip and shake my head no.

"I'm not ready for that Dean, and I don't think I ever will be. I understand that you are healing, like me, but memories still hurt Dean." Dean nods his head in understanding.

"Well, it was nice seeing you again Tally. Good luck, and goodbye." I stand there and watch him walk away.

I head to my car and pull my phone out of my back pocket. I call Scarlett and Cassidy and tell them to meet me at home in an hour. I drive home with thousands of butterflies in my stomach. I'm excited and nervous all at the same time. I hope that James hasn't moved on. Oh God, the thought hit me. What if he is at the wrap party with a date? Should I call him now or wait until the party? It's a few days away, can I hold out that long? Okay, all excitement is now vanished and I'm feeling sick again.

Shit. I pull up at my drive surprised to see Cassidy's car in my drive already. I laugh to myself and get out of my car. I start towards my house and Cass comes bounding out of the door like a golden retriever.

"Oh my God Tally. What the fuck? Why did you meet with Dean fucking Riley? Have you lost your goddamn mind?" I can't help but laugh at all her questions.

"You done? I needed to see him, we talked about everything. He is sorry for what he did. He explained everything to me and I'm happy to move on okay? Now are you going to help me get ready to win my heart back or not?"

It's the day of the wrap party, my nerves are shot. I haven't been online, out of fear of seeing or hearing that James has moved on. Sam and Carlos have been keeping me busy at work so that I don't think too much about him. I feel stupid because it took me so losing James for me to see how much I truly love him. James has my heart, completely.

Scarlett and Cass are in my bedroom discussing how I'm wearing my hair and make-up like. I already have my dress, shoes and bag, courtesy of Scarlett Avenue. The girls turn to look at me like I'm their latest project. Oh shit, I am. I smile to myself. "What are you all smiley about?"

"Just thinking about how you two are going to work your magic on me and make me look fucking hot for James. I just hope it isn't a waste." I shrug. Scarlett comes over to me and grips my face in her hands.

"He loves you and you love him. He is a fucking asshole if he doesn't take you back tonight, okay?" I nod.

"Okay ladies, let's get this party started." Cassidy turns to her iPhone on the docking station and hits play. 'I belong to you' by Paramore plays and I laugh.

Two hours later I'm dressed and primed and ready to go. I stand in front of my full length mirror and study myself. I'm wearing a black strapless dress that stops mid-thigh. The bottom half of the dress is covered in lace. I'm wearing my matching black peep toe shoes. I have no necklace on, but have pretty drop earrings and a few loose bracelets on my right wrist. I'm wearing my sibling ring that Scarlett and Jake bought me.

My hair is down, but curled at the ends and pinned back on one side of my head. Wow, I can't believe I'm going to do this. The girls are sitting in my bed, looking rather proud. I have to say, they have out done themselves. I twirl for them and we all laugh. "Okay Pup, let's get you to that party, shall we?" I nod and breathe out the breath I have been holding. Cassidy hands me my clutch and we all head for the door. Once we step outside, I stop in my tracks and look back at my sister.

"What did you do?" She shrugs and smiles.

"I called in a favor. I thought you could arrive in style, Pup." I look back at the shiny silver Mercedes F800. Wow, that car is the shit. The passenger door opens and my jaw hits the floor. Tanner steps out, looking all sharp and handsome in his black suit. He walks towards me with a huge grin on his beautiful face.

"Oh my God Tanner, is that your car?" I say, waving my hand in the car's direction. He laughs and shakes his head.

"No Tally, this car belongs to Erica. After the phone call I had from your sister, I asked Erica to help out and let me borrow her car for a few hours." I look at the car over his shoulder.

"Erica just let you drive her Merc?" I raise an eyebrow.

"Okay, okay, I begged her. Babe, have you seen that car? It's every boy's wet dream. Plus, I get to drive an absolute stunning lady to a party in it, so that's an added bonus." He offers me his elbow and kisses my cheek. "Your carriage awaits you, chica"

I smile and wave back to my sister and best friend. I mouth 'Thank You' and they both blow me kisses. Tanner opens the door for me and I climb in. I take deep breaths and play with my bag. Tanner walks around the car and folds into the driver seat. He smiles at me. "You ready?" I nod, too afraid to hear my own voice. He starts the car and pulls away from my house while I wave to Scarlett and Cassidy. I owe them so damn much.

We arrive at the club where the wrap party is being held and there are paparazzi everywhere. There are two cars in front of ours, so I get to sit and take it all in. Tanner reaches for my hand. "You will be fine Tally, okay? Just tell James how you feel and things will work out, I believe that." I smile and nod again. Our car moves forward and the butterflies decide to kick in again. I brace myself as we pull up at the red carpet.

Okay, I can do this.

The door opens and I place my hand in the hand offered to me and climb out. Camera flashes are going off to my left and right. Questions are being shouted at me, but I ignore them. I make my way into the club where the doorman gives me a chin lift and allows me to continue through the door. I walk down the dark hall way until I come to a smartly dressed guy with a clip board.

"Name please?" I take a deep breath, praying James didn't remove my name.

"Natalia Slone." I say in a weak voice. He looks down the list and nods to the guy to lift the red rope.

"Enjoy your evening, Miss Slone." I nod and give my thanks.

Chapter 19

I enter the large room with flashing multi coloured lights and loud music playing. I look around the room for James or maybe someone I may know. With no luck, I head for the bar. "Hi, what can I get you?"

"Can I have lemon water please?" The bartender nods and heads off to make my drink. I take my drink and head for a tall stool and tall bar table. I have been here an hour already and not seen anyone I know. I have a sinking feeling in my belly. I don't think tonight will go in my favor. Perhaps James did come with a date and he is with her right now, taking her like he did me. The thought of James touching other women makes my skin crawl and tears burn my eyes at the thought. After another glance around the room, I spot Sasha heading my way. A small, fake smile creeps over my face as she gets closer.

"Oh my, Tally you look outstanding, girl. I'm so glad you came. I thought James said that you weren't coming because of the break up." I try to smile at her, but it's hard to after hearing that James has told people that we had broken up.

"Umm, I wasn't going to come, but I have sorted a few things out and I think that I owe James an explanation. Is he here?" Her smile fades and my heart sinks again. "He has brought a date, hasn't he?"

She gives me a sympathetic smile. "I'm sorry, Tally. I tried to tell him to wait for a while, but you know how strong willed James is." I smile.

"Yeah, I know. Well Sasha, the room looks amazing and I really hope you raise a lot of money tonight. I will be making a donation also. I will get in touch, okay? I'm going to pop to the ladies and then head home. He has moved on, so I guess that's what I have to do again." She hugs me and steps back for me to leave.

I make it to the ladies without any interactions with anyone. A see a few men looking my way, but I ignore them. Scarlett and Cassidy would be proud of their magic. I leave the ladies and head back out across the dance floor and I see him, sitting in a booth with big ass fake titted blond. She has her head buried in his neck, but James is just looking around the room while drinking his drink. He seems uninterested. Why would he bring a date if he didn't want to interact with her?

Fuck, this hurts, though. My stomach knots and my chest constricts. I head across the dance floor towards the door, hoping I can leave before anyone sees my tears. I try not to look at him with Miss Barbie-wanna-be, but I can't help myself. I chance a glance at him and at that exact second, as if he senses me, James turns his head towards me.

Our eyes lock and a tear escapes down my cheek. Shock, guilt and confusion crosses his face. I shake my head and continue wading through the crowd. I can almost see the red rope when I feel a hand on my arm. I don't need to turn around to see James standing behind me. I close my eyes and take a deep soothing breath, trying to calm my sobs. I turn to face him, God he looks good. He is wearing black jeans with a white dress shirt, the sleeves rolled up past the elbow.

"What are you doing here Tally?" I notice a little annoyance in his voice. What the hell? I look away. I can't look at him right now.

"It's doesn't matter, James. I was just leaving. I know when I'm not wanted anymore. You would have thought I would have learned after the last time, right?" I laugh and shake my head. I just can't believe that I thought this would work.

"Answer me Tally. Why are you here?" Anger boils in me and turn to look at him, after everything that has happened between us, he is angry at me. Like fuck.

"I came here to tell you that I love you, I want to be with you." I lower my voice "I went to see Dean." Anger flashes across his face.

"What the fuck Tally!? You went to see that rapist? For fucks sake, he beat and raped you and you went to see him?" I'm shocked by his behavior.

I growl at him. "Keep your fucking voice down, Wilde. This is my life and it's my choice to go to see the man who fucked me up as you so politely put it, then I fucking will." I keep going as he just stands there in shock. "You walked away from me remember, telling me that I didn't love you enough to let you love me. Well James fucking Wilde, I do okay? I fucking love you. It's such a shame that you *didn't* love me enough, as from what I just saw." I nod my head in Miss Barbie's direction. I take a deep breath

"*You* have moved on. Dean really helped me see today how much I love you and how much I need you, but you know what Wilde? *Fuck You*, because I don't need you. Now go back to your new little girlf-" I get cut off my James crashing his lips to mine.

Everything around me fades away, the music, the lights. Even the chatter of people nearby. I am consumed by James's mouth.

I try to push away, but find my body betrays me. My mind and my body melt into his touch. He slips his tongue into my mouth and our tongue's play together. James puts his hands on my ass and lifts me, crashing into the wall behind me. I moan as James trails kisses down my neck and across my collar bone. All my anger slips away and I open my eyes to see a few people looking at us.

Shit I forgot where we were. Oops. "James we need to stop, people are watching us." He lifts his head and kisses my lips slowly and gently.

"Fuck baby, I missed you. God, I love you Tally, always baby. I'm so damn sorry for everything I have put you through. I can be such a dick sometimes. I know these past few weeks haven't been a nice and easy few. I get it, but baby please forgive me." I smile and kiss his nose. "Listen, about my date, my agent told me that it would be a stupid ass move to turn up alone, so he arranged for her to come with me. She is his niece or something. I'm not interested in her baby. She was just a stand in. I haven't done anything with her. Not even a kiss, I promise."

"I believe you James. Just by seeing you in that booth, I could tell you didn't want her. I missed you babe. Like really missed you. We still have a lot to talk about, my head is so screwed with all this emotion from our on and off again. It's giving me whiplash." James gives me his All-American-Smile that I love so damn much. James sets me down on my feet, but never lets me go. "Shall we go back to your wrap party? All these people are here for you, baby." He shakes his head with a smile. "What?"

"I like that you call me baby, you never have." I smile and pull back into the main room.

He wraps his arm around my waist and walks me over to Sasha, who is talking to a couple. My heart skips a beat when I see that the man standing with Sasha is an older version of James. I look up at James, he must have sensed my worry. "Baby, it's my parents. I would love for you to meet them. They will love you, just like I do." I smile nervously as we get closer to his parents. His mom turns around and hugs her son.

"Oh James, there you are honey. We just got here." He kisses her cheek.

"Hi Mom, Dad. There is someone I want you to meet." He looks down at me and smiles proudly "Mom, Dad, this is my girlfriend, Natalia Slone. Tally, these are my parents, Joan and Jonathan Wilde." I smile and offer my hand.

"It's very nice to meet you both." Joan pulls me in for a huge hug. I hear James laugh. I look him and shake my head. Jonathan hugs me next.

"Oh baby girl, look at you. What a beautiful woman you are. It's nice to finally put a beautiful face to a beautiful name." He turns to James. "You did well, son." He winks at me.

"Hey now Dad, no flirting with my girl. Less of the sexy winks please." James winks at me and I laugh.

"All beautiful women deserve to be winked at my boy, ask your Mom." We all laugh.

James drags me around the room introducing me to his 'people', as he calls them. They all worked on 'Control' in some way. I have been dragged around for about three hours, James parents have left to go back to their hotel room.

We are standing by the bar talking to some of the crew when we hear a commotion coming from the main door. I see James's eyes go slightly wide and he looks down at me with a tight smile. "Brace yourself, baby." I frown and turn towards the noise. My eyes land on Scott Martin, striker for LA Galaxy. Fuck no! I turn back to James.

"Shit, baby let me handle them okay? I'll be back." James grips my hips.

"No babe, we will deal with them together. I can only assume that Jake is here also."

I nod and we make our way over to the team. Scott spots me and smiles. "Tally baby, how are you doing? I haven't seen you in weeks." I smile back and except the kiss on my cheek from him.

"New job Scotty, I'm sure Jake has told you that. Where is he, Scotty? I know you all came to back him up, and to size up James. It's what you boys do when I'm concerned."

He shrugs, but before he can answer I hear my brother. "I'm here, Pup." He pats Scott on the shoulder. "I'm good man, go and enjoy the night." Scott leans in and kisses my cheek again. I feel James tense beside me, so I rub his hand that is on my right hip.

"You hurt her again, you deal with the entire Galaxy. You feel me?" He says looking directly at James. I roll my eyes. James nods, but he doesn't seem threatened by Scott. Wait until Jake starts. Scott walks away. The couple of Galaxy boys nod, smile at me, and follow Scotty. I look back at Jake and go to speak, but he raises his hand to stop me.

"I'm your big brother Pup and it's my job to protect you. I have failed epically in the past, but not anymore. I know that you know about what Dean did to her James, but you still hurt her, granted she caused some hurt also." I blink at my brother. Wow, where is this calm and collected Jake coming from? Jake continues. "Now I need you to listen to me very, very carefully James Wilde. TV star or not, you *ever* hurt my baby sister again and I swear to God, I will go balls to the wall on you and beat the living fuck out of you. You get me?" James nods and guilt crosses his face. "Good, because as you can see, Tally has a lot of big brothers looking out for her and they will always protect her just like I will, but it's my blood duty to do so. Now shall we start over?"

I let out my breath, not noticing I was holding it. Jake lifts his hand to James. "Jake Slone, nice to finally meet you." They shake hands and I smile at these two huge men in my life. "Okay, now that all this is sorted I need me some loving. Any single ladies here tonight, Wilde?" I shake my head and laugh.

"Such a man whore, Jakey. Please be good, these people work with James. Please for the love of God, stay the fuck away from the blonde in the red slutty dress okay. She is bad news Jakey. Warn the boys too" Jake pulls me away from James and into his big arms.

"I approve Pup, for now." I smile up at him and kiss his cheek.

"Thank you, Jake. I love you big brother." Jake nods and struts away. We walk around talking to more people and I introduce James to the Galaxy boys. They all get along great, as James used to play soccer.

I yawn and James pulls me tight into his side. "You ready to go baby?" I nod and yawn again. He stands and pulls me over to Sasha.

"We are going Sash, Tally's tired. Give me a text with the final balance, yeah?" He hugs her and kisses her on the cheek. This no longer bothers me, as I know what they mean to each other.

Sasha reaches for me and pulls me into a hugs also. She whispers in my ear. "I'm glad you came this evening. He has been moping around for days. I know you love him and I know that he loves you. He is worth it Natalia." I nod and kiss her cheek. As we make our way through the club and see Marcus head over to us, James stops.

"You two leaving?" asks Marcus. James answers for us.

"Yeah, Tally is tired so we are going to head over to my place." Wow, I haven't been to James's apartment before. Marcus nods, shakes James's hand, and then bends to speak in my ear.

"Thank you for coming back for him. You're good for him Tally. He needs you." He kisses my forehead before pulling away. James shoves his shoulder playfully

"Fuck off dude, stop whispering in my girlfriend's ear. Get your own girl." I laugh and place my hand on James chest while he tightens his grip on my waist.

"See you later guys." Marcus says then turns and walks off into the crowd.

"To my place then?" He smirks.

"Yep" I say, popping the p. James laughs and pulls me towards the door.

I'm surprised again that the paparazzi are still hanging around. We have to walk back down the red carpet to get to James's limo. The flashes start and the questions get thrown at us. James stops smack bang in the middle of the walkway. He turns fully to me and winks.

Oh God, no.

James has one hand on my ass. He pushes the other into my hair and kisses me, not a sweet, gentle kiss, no, but a full devouring kiss, tongue and all. I can feel my body heat from both James and embarrassment. James ends our kiss and smiles at me.

"There, now everyone will know you belong to me baby and I belong to you. Always." I shake my head. James stands tall and proud and makes his announcement "Yes Natalia Slone is my girlfriend and I am truly, madly and deeply in love with her. I am officially off the market ladies." I can't stop laughing. It's so typical of a Hollywood actor to make such a bold statement.

We climb into our waiting limo and head to James's apartment. The limo pulls away from the club. James pulls me into his lap and takes my lips in an intense kiss.

I lick his lips and suck his bottom lip into my mouth which earns me a deep, throaty groan from James, which makes me even hotter.

My skirt is now sitting around my hips and James is running his hands up and down my thighs. His hands run up my thigh and curve around to cup my ass. I can feel him tug on my panties slightly and then the sound of ripping material makes me gasp. James just tore my panties right off me and again stuffs them into his pants pocket.

Fuck that is *hot*. "I can't wait to be inside of you again, baby. It's been way too long." I reach down to undo his pants button and zipper, while James is kissing and sucking on my neck, sending shivers all down my body.

"Up baby." James lifts his hips slightly so I can pull his pants down along with his boxers, his erection springs free, ready and waiting. God how I have missed him so much, but it dawns on me, has James been with anyone else since we have been apart? The blond was all over him. Is she one of many? I jerk back from James and see the confusion on his face.

"Baby what's wrong? Are we going too fast?" My heart rate picks up speed. I need to ask, but I'm also afraid to.

"James, since we have been broken up ummm...Have you been with anyone else? I'm sorry, but I have to ask." I look down at my hands and twist my ring.

I feel James's thumb and forefinger lift my chin, so I'm looking at his beautiful face. "Tally I have only ever been with you in any way shape or form since that first night at JAG, okay?" I nod.

"I know you haven't touched that blond back there, but was there other dates that you touched? It hurts to ask, but I have to." I can feel tears building. Wow, talk about a cold bucket on your sex drive. He shakes his head .

"No-one Tally, I mean it okay? No-one." He emphasises the word 'No-one'. I nod and smile at him. James wipes a stray tear that runs down my cheek and pulls my head to his chest. His erection still free and between us, but still very much ready and waiting.

"How long until we arrive at you're place?" James looks out the window.

"About fifteen minutes, why? What do you have in mind baby?" I smile slyly and slide off James's lap. I kneel between his legs and wink at him as I take his cock in my hand. I slowly run my hand up and down that produces a small bead of pre-cum at his tip. He is watching me like a hawk and it makes me feel powerful to have him at my mercy. I lick the tip of his dick and he moans my name.

"Suck it Tally. Take it all baby. I have waited too long to have your sweet mouth wrapped around me again." I part my swollen lips and run my tongue from root to tip of his shaft. James hips buck so I do it again. I smile to myself and take him full into my mouth. I suck softly at first, but I hear James breath catch so I suck harder, running my tongue along underneath him. He tastes so good. I don't think I will ever get enough of him.

James places his hand on my head and adds a little pressure, but not too much to make me gag. I feel it hit the back of my throat and he groans louder this time. I don't care that we are in the back of his limo, that the driver's just behind the screen, or that people are just outside the car.

Another moan from James and I smile up at his through my eyelashes. "Baby I need to be inside you, like yesterday." I chuckle as James pulls me up his body and gives me his panty-dropping smile. "Ride me Tally." Oh God, I don't need to be told twice. I lift myself up and James positions his cock at my entrance, he runs the head of his cock over my wetness, teasing me. I slide down slowly, inch by inch. "Fuck baby, you feel so damn good." We both moan in unison. My head falls back as I start to move up and down his length.

James pulls my dress down over my breasts and takes one of my nipples into his hot mouth. "James I need to come. Please baby, make me come." He sucks harder, so I move faster and harder.

"Yeah Tally, just like that. Ride me baby. Harder Tally, *harder.*" His voice strains with pleasure. I do what he says and I slam back down on him and ride him. Fuck I can feel my muscles tighten. James bucks his hips once more and I explode around him. My orgasm yet again sets James's off and we both come hard. Panting heavy into James chest I try to catch my breath while smiling to myself. I look up at my Hollywood-super-star boyfriend and smile.

"All mine Mr Wilde, all mine" He gives me killer smile.

"Yeah baby, all yours." I take a deep breath and lay my head back on his chest. James runs his hand up and down my back. I hear him whisper, "

You gonna let me love you, Tally Slone?"

"Yes James Wilde, I will let you love me."

Epilogue

Tally

I'm standing in the full length mirror in James's bedroom, well I should say, 'our bedroom'. The night James and I got back together, he asked me to move in with him. He told me that he was never letting me go again and he has been true to his word. I moved my things in over the next few days. I have lived with James for five months now.

Tonight is finally Scarlet's birthday party, the big three-0. I'm in a dress that Scarlet picked out for me. It's champagne in color with a thin pink ribbon around the waist. It comes just above my knee. I'm in baby pink heels that I'm actually able to walk in. My hair is straightened, but with two sections pulled back to meet at the back of my head. I'm wearing my sibling ring again, as I never take it off. I'm also wearing a new diamond earring set with a matching necklace and bracelet that James bought me as a moving in present.

I hear James coming towards the bedroom and brace myself for what he will look like. After all this time, he still takes my breath away when he enters the room. I turn towards the door and my man is there leaning against door frame. "Hi baby." I smile at him.

"Fuck Tally, you look simply stunning. But you know...that dress would look so much better on the floor right about now." I laugh and shake my head.

"God James, you have sex on the brain twenty-four-seven. You're a pervert, Mr. Wilde." He steps closer to me, wraps his arms around my waist, and kisses my neck.

"Yes baby, but I'm your pervert. Am I right?" He trails butterfly kisses along my neck and across my bare shoulder.

"James stop, do you want to tell Scarlett why we are late?" He reluctantly pulls away, as he knows what tonight means to my sister. He takes my hand and leads me downstairs and out to his car. It takes us around forty-five minutes to get to the club where Scarlett is having her party. Her party is being held at Club Blue. James pulls up outside, hands his keys to the valet, and opens my door, offering me his hand. "Thank you, babe."

I smile and kiss his cheek. There are a few cameras going off, as it was leaked about tonight's party. The room looks fantastic. White fairy lights are everywhere; it looks like a frozen fairyland. There are a large number of people here, from family to close friends. Jake's soccer team is here with their wives and girlfriends. They look very handsome in their tuxedos.

I see Charlie and give him a little wave. He still has yet to meet James, unlike half of the team. I pull James towards him. "Hey Charlie. I haven't seen you in a while. How have you been, bud?" We hug and he kisses my cheek.

"Ah, you know, Pup. The season is off to a great start, so we train to keep up the pace, you know?" I nod in understanding. I turn to my boyfriend.

"James, this is Charlie Daniels. He plays on Jake's team and is a very good friend of mine. Charlie, this is my sexy as sin boyfriend, James Wilde"

They shake hands and nod. "So you're the guy who broke our Pup's heart? You know she was devastated?" I look to Charlie. I go to speak, but James gets in there first.

"I am, but now I'm the guy who owns her heart and I do not intend to break it ever again. I know I hurt her in the past, but never again. I know you look out for her Charlie and I'm grateful that she has you as another big brother, so I thank you for looking after my girl when I didn't." I gawk at James and look back to Charlie. James offers his hand again and Charlie takes it. *Wow.* I say bye to Charlie and go look for the birthday girl.

I spend a few hours walking around the room, introducing James to my family and friends. Cassidy and Josh are here. Lucas is here with what we call a 'freaking miracle'. Lucas has been dating the same girl, Katie, for the last three weeks. I see Ella and Marie, Ella still eyefucking my brother. She needs to make a move soon. Also, all my Exposure family are here. My brother Jake taps me on the shoulder. "It's time, Pup" I turn to him and nod.

The artist Scarlett hired turned out to be Ne-Yo, which by the way I *love*. Ne-Yo finishes his set and now the DJ has the floor. "James I need to go up on stage okay? I will be back soon." He kisses the top of my head and I follow Jake to the stage to sing Happy Birthday to my sister.

"Ladies and gents can I have your attention please?" My dad speaks up and the crowd settles. "You all know that we are here to celebrate Scarlett's thirtieth birthday. She has done an amazing job with this party, the room looks fantastic. I would like to thank you all for coming and spending this night with us in celebration. What a celebration it shall be." My dad looks at me and winks. I smile and let it pass over my head. Scarlett steps forwards and kisses our dad.

"Like my dad just said, thank you all for spending tonight with me. You are all very special to me. Now tonight is not only about me. I have been asked to share my night with another special occasion."

I frown at my sister as she, my parents, and my brother back off the stage. I go to follow, but I feel someone touch my elbow. I turn and James is standing there with a big ass smile on his face.

"Baby, what are you doing?" I look back and forth between James and my family.

"Tally, from the first time I laid my eyes on you in JAG, I knew that you would be in my life for a very long time. We have had a rocky path to get where we are, but I'm glad that we are here today. I asked you to let me love you and you did. That day was the best day of my life. I will always 'Live and Breathe' you Natalia, always. Nate showed me how to live on and not waste a single second of life."

I can't breathe. James is still holding my hands when he goes down on one knee. He lets one hand go, only to produce a little white velvet box. Oh my God. I can't take my eyes off it. "Natalia Grace Slone, please would you do me the honor of letting me love you for the rest of our lives by becoming my wife?"

I gasp and nod my head. "Baby, I need to hear you say it." The tears are free flowing now, but I smile at my husband-to-be.

"Yes James, I will let you love me for the rest of our lives, as long as I can love you until the end of time." James stands and kisses me with all his power. I look down at my ring and its simple, it's very me. It's a white gold band with a square diamond seated on top. That's not the best part. James removes my ring and shows me the side of the ring. In very delicate white gold there are two wings connected in the center. I gasp and twist my sibling ring.

"Baby I know how much your sibling ring means to you." He plays with my sibling ring. "I wanted to add the wings to my ring for you also. I hope that's okay." I nod and kiss him again. It doesn't matter that all my family and friends are cheering. There is only me and James at the moment in our little bubble. I feel more hands on me and I pull from James's lips to see my parents and brother and sister. We all hug.

I turn to Scarlett. "Sorry if we stole all your thunder. James should have waited." I turn my head to James, who is talking to my father and brother. I'm so happy to see the three main men in my life getting along.

"I wanted this to be special for you, Pup. Nothing will top tonight. There is nothing that can make this night better." I smile and shrug. Scarlett catches on. She knows I'm keeping something from her.

"What is it?" I shake my head.

"James, come here babe." James makes his way over to me. "I know that tonight is Scarlett's birthday and now the announcement that James and I are engaged, but there is something else that needs to be said." I hear my mom gasp and cover her mouth with her hand.

"James, you know I love you always?" He nods and looks slightly confused. "I went to see my doctor last week, as I was feeling run down, but I thought it was stress from work. They ran some tests and they told me umm...I'm pregnant James. I'm ten weeks pregnant." I hear gasps all around me, but can't take my eyes off of James. Minutes pass and I start to freak out inside. He looks me dead in the eyes.

"I'm going to be a dad?" I nod, too scared to smile. I huge smile spreads across James's face "I'm going to be a dad? Fuck baby. That's fucking fantastic. Oh my God, a Baby Wilde." He smirks and places his hand over my belly.

A happy James Wilde. I smile to myself.

James
Three years later

I stand by the pool bar and watch my wife chat to her sister, Scarlett. You heard right, my wife. I can't help but get a hard-on. You would think that after being together for four years, the effect she has on me would wear off, but nope. She gets my blood pumping just by smiling at me.

"Hey dude. Great party, even if it is a kid's party." Marcus, my best friend and also my soon-to-be brother-in-law says. Yep you got it, he and Scarlett got together just after her birthday party. He was also my best man on the day I married Tally.

"Hey. Glad you're enjoying yourself." I say, laughing. I hear girly screams and I look towards to pool. Jake is throwing my daughter in the air and catching her before she goes under the water. My baby girl Everly has mousey brown coloured hair like me, but is a double image of her mom. I'm going to have trouble when she gets older.

While I'm watching Jake toss Everly in the water, I see Marcus bend down to pick up Nate, my son. Yep that's right, Tally and I had twins. We had a shock when we went to have a sonogram done and they told us that we were having twins.

We didn't wait too long to get married, as Tally didn't want to look too big in our wedding photos. So, we opted for a small gathering at a celebrity friend's beach house.

It was secluded and very private. It was very casual. I wore a white linen shirt and pants with no shoes. Tally wanted bare feet. Tally wore a simple ivory strapless dress designed by a designer who sells via Scarlett Avenue. Tally chose ivory and baby pink gerbera flowers. She wore a pink gerbera in her hair. My wife looked fucking beautiful.

We didn't find out the sex of the babies, as we wanted a surprise. Nathan Jake Wilde is just three minutes older than his sister Everly Scarlett Wilde. We named Nate after my brother and Tally wanted her brother and sisters names in our kid's names as well. "Hey little dude. Are you having fun?" Nate poked Marcus in the nose.

"Yep Uncle Mac. Tank you for my cars." I laugh at Nate's attempt at 'Thank You'. Marcus asked for Nate and Everly to call him Uncle Mac, as they were having trouble saying Marcus.

"No worries, kiddo. Glad you like them. What do you say we go over and chat to Auntie Scar for a bit, yeah?" Nate nods with a huge grin on his face. He loves his Auntie Scar, as she spoils my kids rotten.

I stand there and watch my best friend walk off with my son. As soon as Marcus and Nate make it to the girls, Tally heads my way. I smile my sexy ass smile that I know she loves.

"Hey baby. You okay?" I ask her when she stops in front of me. Tally wraps her arms around my neck and pulls me in for a kiss. Fuck me. I'm getting hard again. "Baby stop, I don't fancy showing people that my sexy as fuck wife is turning me on." She smiles her sweet smile.

"I missed, you that's all. I needed to touch you again. Nothing wrong with that, is there?" She runs her hand down from my neck to my dick and rubs me through my shorts. She tries to look all innocent. Yeah, I'm not buying that.

"You had me this morning, Tally. Baby you seem horny all the time. The last time you where like this was when-"I stop and I pull back and look at her. She shrugs and smiles. "You're fucking with me?" I ask her. She bites her bottom lip and shakes her head no.

"Nope, I found out yesterday. I'm six weeks pregnant Wilde. Let's just hope it isn't twins this time."

I have always lived by the motto as stated on my rib tattoo "Live & Breathe"

That's what Nate and I used to say when he was ill. I messed up for a while a few years back, but not anymore. After the birth of the twins I added three stars to my right shoulder for three more important people in my life. I also have Natalia tattooed in a fine script across my heart, right where she belongs. Tally decided to get inked also. She had my name tattooed on the inside of her right wrist. Tally also has wings between her shoulder blades with Nate and Everly's initials in each one.

I have an amazingly beautiful wife, who I know Nate would have loved. I have two of the most awesome kids a dad could ask for. Nate would have loved being an Uncle to Nate and Everly and now my wife has just told me we are expecting another baby. What more can an Award winning Hollywood TV star want?

Natalia Slone finally let me love her and I do it with all my heart and soul.

The End

Also available
Phoenix Series
Rafe
Ryder
Reeve

The phoenix boys are triplet's who are in college in Long Beach, California. But also are in a rock band Inside Noise.

They grew up in the music industry and they have the whole rock star package.

Each boy finds love but can they hold onto it, they all have their issues but will they overcome them? Things get in their way but they push through and make the most of life.

'Live, Love, take it to the stage and party like a rock star' that's the Phoenix Boys motto.

Acknowledgements

Again a big thank you to my husband Darryl, you are my rock.
A big thank you to my Beta reader's. Without you girls I don't know if this book would have ever been published.
Sarah Jayne, Katie Nicholls, Beccy Hanford, Michelle Carroll.
and Kirsty Moseley (Ok people you need to check out these ladies books. EPIC)
#TeamLiam
Thank you for taking the taking the time to read James.
Also a huge thank you to the blog pages that have taken the time to read James and leave a review
Also a HUGE Thank you to my chickpea Kellie Montgomery and my Angel Sarah Jayne, plus Carrie and Toski over at
Eye Candy Bookstore
Facebook.com/EyeCandyBookstore

Please if you enjoyed this book, I would be so grateful if you could leave a review on Amazon and Goodreads please.
Thank You for reading my debut book.
Amy x

Facebook.com/AmyDaviesBooks
AmyDaviesBooks@gmail.com

A bit about the author

Amy is a 32 year old mum who lives in South Wales, UK with her husband and three children. She has been a stay at home mam since having the 3 children and as she is an avid reader she decided to have a go at writing her own book.

Amy has a weakness for hardcore biker boys and rockstars. But also the sweet cowboys. Who doesn't right?

With the support and family and friends, some she hasn't even met in person yet, James and Tally's story was born.

Made in the USA
Middletown, DE
28 February 2019